# ENTER THE NYCTALOPE

# ENTER THE NYCTALOPE

by
**Jean de La Hire**

Translated by
**Brian Stableford**

A Black Coat Press Book

Visit our website at www.blackcoatpress.com

ISBN 978-1-934543-99-3. First Printing. July 2009. Published by Black Coat Press, an imprint of Hollywood Comics.com, LLC, P.O. Box 17270, Encino, CA 91416. All rights reserved. Except for review purposes, no part of this book may be reproduced or transmitted in any form or by any means, electronic or mechanical, including photocopying, recording, or by any information storage and retrieval system, without permission in writing from the publisher. The stories and characters depicted in this novel are entirely fictional. Printed in the United States of America.

# Table of Contents

# ENTER THE NYCTALOPE

## Part One: The End of Darkness

### *Chapter I: The Drama*

When he woke up on the morning of March 3, 1912, the engineer Pierre Saint-Clair felt his heart gripped by an obscure anguish. It was a presentiment that the day would not pass without some misfortune befalling him.[1]

He was reassured however, at 8 a.m., when Mélanie, his old cook-housekeeper, brought him a telegram announcing the arrival, before noon on that same day, of Madame Saint-Clair and their son Léon, whom they called Leo. On the previous day, Madame Saint-Clair and Leo had gone to Chartres by automobile, in order to deliver their birthday greetings to an old uncle. Monsieur Saint-Clair had not been able to accompany them because he had had to work late into the night on a very important laboratory experiment.

---

[1] Both the year in which the story is supposed to take place and the first name of the Nyctalope's father are discussed at some length in the afterword.

For more than a year, in fact, the engineer had devoted all his time and the greater part of the income from his fortune to the realization of an invention of immense potential. That invention consisted of an electromagnetic wave "captoprojector" capable of attracting and, so to speak, storing wireless telegraphy waves, and subsequently liberating then, authentically or in a falsified form. Result: absolute mastery of all the wireless telegraphy communications in the entire world, by means of a permanent control enabling censorship, transformation, delay and even suppression.

The science and applications of wireless telegraphy were then in their infancy, and the scientist anticipated their marvelous progress.

The Saint-Clairs lived in a fine family property between Paris and Bourg-la-Reine, comprising a comfortable house, grounds enclosed by high walls, and vast commons. The engineer had installed his laboratory—a workshop-shed and an experimental field—in the middle of the grounds, in a large clearing surrounded by tall trees. He worked alone, but his twenty-year-old son Leo, who was intelligent and devoted, sometimes served as his enthusiastic assistant. The young man had just been awarded a degree in science, but he was a combative and ambitious sportsman and was still hesitating over the choice of a career.

One the morning of March 3, 1912, therefore, Saint-Clair was reassured by the thought that his wife and son would be returning on that day, and not—as might have been the case—the following day. At 10 a.m., he was in his laboratory, hard at work, satisfied and triumphant. He had just completed the definitive experiment in the most fortunate manner when the private telephone connecting the laboratory to the house sounded its silvery bell.

Monsieur Saint-Clair uncooked the receiver and said: "Hello?"

"Hello, Monsieur!" replied the easily-recognizable voice of Mélanie. "Antoine has asked me to tell you that there's a gentleman asking to see you." Antoine was the Saint-Clairs' gardener, a faithful old retainer who lived in a little lodge beside the gate at the entrance to the property.

"The gentleman has given Antoine a card, which he has just handed to me," Mélanie continued. "His name is Stanislas Vibrosky. He's a chemist. He says that he has traveled from the depths of Poland for the express purpose of seeing you."

Monsieur Saint-Clair knew the name Stanislas Vibrosky, of whom he had, indeed, heard mention as a very knowledgeable chemist. He had even seen his picture several times in illustrated periodicals. Furthermore, he often received visits from foreign scientists, for "the engineer Saint-Clair" was world-famous by virtue of several inventions related to electricity, radiography, radiophony, and wireless telegraphy in general. In consequence, the engineer's suspicions were not aroused.

As he always did in such cases, he replied; "That's all right, Mélanie. Tell Antoine to let Monsieur Vibrosky in, to take him to my study and ask him to wait for a few minutes."

He hung up the telephone and went back to work. In fact, he required nearly a quarter of an hour of material manipulations and note-taking to finish off the definitive experiment and to consign the final formula and its technical consequences to his "Radiant Z Journal." When that was done, he left the apparatus and the Journal where they were on the large steel laboratory table and went into the study.

The latter was a room of restricted dimensions, furnished as a library and smoking-room, and equipped with three good armchairs. Saint-Clair used it for resting, meditation and reading, and also for receiving visitors when he was in his "Workshops." The laboratory was connected to the study by a short corridor with two doors. Between the two doors the corridor served as a cloakroom for coats and hats. The study was entered from the outside by a separate door opening on to a wide pathway that led directly to the house.

On entering the study, however, Monsieur Saint-Clair experienced a sharp surprise. The man who was standing there waiting for him, whose face was clearly lit from the side by the room's only window, was not recognizable as the Stanislas Vibrosky of the printed portraits. Abruptly, with a vague chill running along his spine, the dark presentiment he had experienced on awakening came back. Instinctively, he took a step backwards, on his guard—but it was already too late!

Violent and terrible, the drama unfolded. It began with a gesture from the stranger and a rapid speech. The gesture consisted of the man raising his right hand and aiming the Browning with which it was armed at Monsieur Saint-Clair. As for the speech, it was as menacing as the gesture, and just as frightfully significant.

"Monsieur Saint-Clair," the false Vibrosky pronounced, in a harsh tone, with an accent that was certainly that of some Far-Eastern nation, "you will immediately give me the complete dossier of your Radiant Z, and you will follow me to the automobile that is waiting for you on the road outside the gate of the property. If not…"

Monsieur Saint-Clair stiffened, put his hand on the back of a chair that he thought might serve as a weapon, and said, courageously: "If not?"

The response was immediate. His green eyes shining with an evil gleam, the stranger said: "If not, whatever the consequences might be, I'll kill you."

Monsieur Saint-Clair was agile and vigorous. He thought quickly and acted promptly. He crouched down, while gripping the chair with both hands, and raised it in the air—but he was dealing with a coldly determined criminal aggressor. Before the raised chair could strike him, the stranger pulled the trigger of his weapon. Three detonations were heard, but they were soft and feeble, because the Browning was equipped with one of those so-called "silencers," which are little used although they are genuinely effective, considerably diminishing the sound of a rifle- or pistol-shot. Those three detonations would not even have been heard by anyone who happened to be in the neighboring laboratory.

The unfortunate Monsieur Saint-Clair collapsed, and the chair fell back upon his own body.

Without sparing his victim a glance, the criminal leapt forward and shoved the corridor door, which still stood ajar. He opened the door to the laboratory, ran to the steel table, set down his still-smoking Browning on a corner, and began riffling through Saint-Clair's "Radiant Z Journal" with both hands. His Mongoloid face, with slanting eyes and prominent cheek-bones, wore an expression of ferocious joy as he sniggered.

"This is it!" he growled. "It's all here. It's ours—and it will be ours alone, for my little time-bombs will destroy all this in a quarter of an hour. And in a quarter of an hour, I'll be far away, since the car will get me to the airplane in less than five minutes. Hup! Let's not waste any time."

The criminal was wearing a raglan overcoat with large, deep pockets. Into one of them he slid the bound notebook constituting the "Radiant Z Journal;" in the other he buried two items of apparatus, with disks and reels, which had also been on the table. Then he picked up the Browning in his right hand.

He took a small square box from the left-hand outside pocket of his raglan, and put it under a stool. He scraped a fingernail over one of its surfaces, thus exposing the head of a pin that had previously been hidden beneath a thin layer of plaster. He pulled out the pin, and threw it away.

He left the laboratory immediately by the back door and passed into a large work-room. There he placed four little boxes in different places and removed their pins. Finally, he went out on to the lawn, went around the buildings at a rapid pace, rejoined the wide pathway, went around the house and headed for the gate along a path slanting from the right.

As he came out of the bushes he saw that the gate was open and that Antoine, standing beside one of the battens, was waving to a red cabriolet that was going past him into the grounds, launching itself into the central pathway with the forceful acceleration that only first-class motors can achieve.

"Good!" muttered the fake Vibrosky. "Here's Madame Saint-Clair and her son coming home. Our information was accurate. I've arrived just in time, and I'll wager that it's the perfect moment. There's no time for delay." And as Antoine, who was about to close the gate again, looked at him, the stranger said: "*Au revoir*, my good man."

Bewildered by such rare generosity, Antoine contemplated the hundred-franc note that the visitor had just slipped into his hand. When he raised his head again and looked at the road, the stranger and his car had disappeared.

## Chapter II: Ah, Youth, Beautiful Youth!

"Is Monsieur in the Workshops, Mélanie?" asked Madame Saint-Clair as she got out of the red cabriolet, which her son was driving.

"Yes, Madame."

"Good!" exclaimed Leo, closing the car door. "I'll go on there."

He declutched, changed gear, and re-engaged the clutch magisterially—and the powerful car, drawing away without and shock, rolled like a supple streak of lightning along the broad rectilinear pathway that led from the house to the Factory.

Leo stopped in front of the large laboratory door and got out. Not seeing his father in the laboratory, however, he crossed the immense room at a rapid pace and went straight to the study.

"Oh, my God! What's happened? Oh, Father, Father!" He had immediately caught sight of the extended body, with the chair overturned on the legs and the arms outstretched, the face livid and bloody... although the eyes were wide open and very much alive!

Leo Saint-Clair was a tall, strapping lad with a steady heart, a clear mind and a courageous character. Although his soul was very sensitive, he was endowed with a magnificently cool head. He had an intuition of what had happened and a fugitive idea of its causes and goals, but he did not waste time with such thoughts.

His eyes were brimming with the tears of a violent and dolorous emotion, but he acted nevertheless with an admirable presence of mind. *Take care of him*, he said to himself. *First, take care of him—but there's none of what's necessary here. The house... the house, quickly!* And he added, with infinite tenderness: "Father, can you hear me? Yes? Good. Don't talk. I'll carry you to the house. I can see that you're wounded in the chest. I'll do it gently."

He had been a scout, and a renowned patrol-leader. He how to take a wounded man in his arms, lift him up and transport him. The captain of Bourg-la-Reine Rugby Club, he was strong and lithe. He could seat his father in the cabriolet...

Less than five minutes later, Pierre Saint-Clair was on the divan in the house's large drawing-room. Madame Saint-Claire, tearful but courageous, forcing herself to remain calm, exposed his breast in order to administer first aid. Mélanie went upstairs in search of the large box of medical supplies, and Leo telephoned Doctor Champeau at Bourg-la-Reine, a friend of his father's and a very skillful physician.

It was then that five distinct detonations rang out in the grounds, one after another, at intervals of a few seconds. The five principal bangs were accompanied by a thunderous racket.

The Workshops could only been seen from the house along the central pathway bordered by linden trees. Through a window looking out in that direction, Leo saw a distant chaos of debris, smoke and fire. Although trembling with emotion, pain and anger, he maintained his presence of mind; he was already at the telephone, giving the alarm to the firemen of Bourg-la-Reine and Arcueil-Cachan.

What a day!

That evening, however, as dusk fell, the situation was clear.

Leo summarized the various aspects of the situation for his friends from the Rugby Club, Robert Champeau, René Croqui and Jean Degains, who had hastened in response to his summons in mid-afternoon and who were dining with him at the house—an undercooked meal served by a tearful and frightened Mélanie.

He was very pale, but steadfast, his gestures precise and his voice level; his entire being emanated a formidable resolution and determination. "My friends," he said, "let's get straight to the point! I've called you together to make some decisions. This is how it is. Firstly, my father. A single bullet struck him, going straight through his chest between the lungs, the heart and the stomach, without injuring any of those vital organs—but it grazed the spinal column. Your father, Robert, is certain that he'll recover, after several months of daily treatment, but he's afraid that a partial paralysis, whose precise location and limits he's unable to specify as yet, might be unavoidable, because of the injury to the spine. I intend to avenge my father, my friends!"

Making an effort to contain the emotion that was making him shiver, Leo Saint-Clair summed after a brief pause: "Secondly, the invention, Radiant Z. You know what it is. You're the only ones I've told, with my father's authorization. Well, the criminal has stolen the plans, drawings, instructions and technical notes relating to the invention. He's also stolen the two scale-models of the apparatus. Finally, he's destroyed the laboratory, the work-room, and everything precious and useful relative to Radiant Z that the Workshops contained. Now, my friends, I intend to get back everything that this criminal has stolen!"

There was another pause, untroubled by Robert Campeau, René Croqui or Jean Degains, who were very emotional and passionately attentive. Then Leo Saint-Clair continued, still with the same concentrated energy.

"Thirdly, and finally, the criminal! Having found or stolen one of the distinguished Polish chemist Stanislas Vibrosky's visiting cards, the bandit has only left us impressions of his face, his build and his accent—impressions graven in my father's memory. When my father was able to talk, he described the physical appearance of the murder to me while I stood at his bedside: Mongoloid face, medium height, thick-set, broad shoulders; a rough, harsh voice with a strange accent, which is none of the accents that Europeans have when they speak French. And one precious item of information, one particular clue: my father noticed, unthinkingly but unmistakably, that the murderous bandit, the mysterious thieving spy, had a horizontal scar on his forehead, directly above the nose and very close to the hairline, cutting across the dull yellow complexion of his facial skin with its livid pallor. The spy kept his hat on, but the abrupt movement he made as he aimed the Browning displaced it slightly and tipped it slightly backwards, thus uncovering the forehead, so that my father's eyes saw the scar and his memory registered its appearance permanently. My friends, I intend to find that man!"

As he made that final statement, proffered with violence, Leo Saint-Clair rose to his feet. His friends immediately followed suit.

Standing up straight, tense and determined, Leo added, rapidly: "I've inherited a considerable sum of money from my maternal grandmother. I'm sure that my father, on my request, will put it at my disposal. Furthermore, if I ask them in my father's name, my dear friends, your relatives—who loved and admired him—will permit you to interrupt your studies as I shall interrupt mine. Why? In order that all four of us can devote ourselves, from this day forward, to a mission of justice and patriotism: to recover Radiant Z and give it to France, and to capture the murderous spy and have him punished. Are you with me? Do you feel that you have the strength and courage to undertake long and perhaps difficult journeys? To brave a thousand dangers? To run risks that might be terrible, and even mortal?"

Leo Saint-Clair had no need to go on. Acting as one, Champeau, Croqui and Degains threw themselves upon him, seized him by the hands and arms, their eyes filled with tears of emotion and enthusiasm, and cried in unison: "Yes! Yes! We'll go with you!"

"We won't just be working for France, but also for Europe!" Leo Saint-Clair went on, more calmly. "For the assassin-spy is neither German, nor English, nor Italian. He's a Mongol, an Asian. For whose profit has he carried out such an abominable and audacious crime? For Germany? We shall find out—but I have an intuition that he might be in the service of enemies of civilization and European peace, of our religious faith and of our magnificent French grandeur: the Russo-Asiatic nihilists!"

Young as they were—between 18 and 20 years of age—Robert Champeau, René Croqui and Jean Degains knew enough about the great events of modern history not to be unaware that the nihilists, bloody conspirators in Russia who aspired to disturb the entire world, were indeed quite capable of wanting to take possession of the marvelous instrument of war and victory that Radiant Z might be, in order to turn Europe and Asia upside-down. Their minds and hearts were, therefore, as one with the mind and heart of their leader and friend Leo Saint-Clair—and like Leo, in an atmosphere of intense emotion, they raised their right hands with their arms extended, and pronounced after him the oath that sprang from his entire being:

"I swear to dedicate all my life's strength to the mission that I accept today, March 3, 1912!"

And they gripped one another in a fraternal embrace. Ah, how young they were! And how beautiful their youth was!

## Chapter III: On the Track

On the next day, March 4, having received permission from Doctor Champeau to listen and talk a little, Pierre Saint-Clair listened to his son Leo and talked to him. He gave the necessary instructions to a hastily-summoned notary, and signed a power of attorney. From then on, Leo Saint-Clair was free to dispose of his personal fortune and had his father's authorization to act on his behalf.

Doctor Champeau and the parents of René Croqui and Jean Degains, who had also come to the house in Bourg-la-Reine, gave their own sons the same authorization that Monsieur and Madame Saint-Clair had given Leo.

That afternoon, Doctor Champeau and the four young men were granted an audience with Monsieur Matot de Passins, the senior assistant to the Minister of Foreign Affairs. Very anxiously, he immediately made the necessary provisions for the four Frenchmen to be amicably received by the ambassadors and consuls of France, on the presentation of a special card that each of them was given, and to be provided with official support and aid.

After this interview, which was of capital importance, Doctor Champeau and the four friends had another, no less important, with the colonel in charge of the Counter-Espionage Service at the Ministry of War. With a very lively interest and evident anxiety, the Colonel listened to the account of events given to him by Leo Saint-Clair. He did not interrupt the young man once.

After a moment's reflection, the Colonel smiled and said: "I'm happy for your family and France that we can count on the recovery, at least partial, of your father, whom we hold in the highest esteem, with great admiration. Furthermore, I congratulate you and your comrades on having conceived the mission to which you are devoting yourselves body and soul—and I can inform you straight away that I can help you in two ways."

"Oh, Colonel!" exclaimed Leo Saint-Clair, slightly reassured for the first time in 24 hours.

"One of the two ways," the officer went on, "is the one on which you counted in coming to my office with Doctor Champeau. Yes, I will give you an encoded list of my foreign secret agents. Yes, I shall give you the key to our secret alphabet and our special signals. Yes, finally, I will recommend you to all our attachés in our embassies and consulates."

This time, the four young men manifested their joy and gratitude in unison, by the expression in their eyes and their entire physiognomy.

After a brief pause, however, the Colonel continued. "I'll wager that the second manner in which I can help you is unexpected. Here it is—read this aloud, my young friend." Swiftly opening a file that was on his desk-top, among others, the officer took out a sheet of paper, which he held out.

Trembling with curiosity, Leo Saint-Clair seized the piece of paper and, in a voice vibrant with emotion, read what was written on it, amid general attention.

*"Confidential report of agent C88, March 3, 1912. This morning, at 7 a.m., as I chanced to be going through my neighborhood, the Porte d'Orléans, I suddenly found myself in the presence of a man whom I recognized as a spy and Russian nihilist of Mongol origin,*

known as Sadi Khan, who is believed sometimes to use a false passport in the name of Theodore Wallis, citizen of the United States residing in Chicago. He was in a limousine, which stopped momentarily and immediately moved off again. I was, however, able to see and note down the number of the car: 6810 HD. It disappeared along the Route d'Orléans in the direction of Arcueil-Cachan. I was unable to follow it immediately, but, Sadi Khan being considered dangerous, I left Paris as soon as possible, at 10 a.m. I made inquiries in the direction of Arcueil-Cachan, Bourg-la-Reine, etc., having learned from the Prefecture of Police that the hire-car 6810 HD belonged to a garage-owner from Antony recently arrived from Tours, where he had followed the same trade.

"My inquiries also took me to Antony. I saw the garage-owner, Monsieur Debalto, who informed me that the car had just been returned. The driver was still there. His name is Adrien Motte. On interrogation, Motte told me the following story, which I took down in shorthand:

" 'I picked up the client with the Chinese face on the Boulevard Brune, 200 meters from the crossroads at the Porte d'Orléans. He told me to take him to the Chemin des Fresnes in Bourg-la-Reine, to the house of the engineer Saint-Clair. I was familiar with the house, for Monsieur Pierre Saint-Clair is very well-known throughout the region. I therefore went to the address in question, and stopped outside the gate for about 20 minutes, waiting for my client, who seemed to be visiting Monsieur Saint-Clair.

" 'When he returned to my car, my client shouted: "To Fresnes Prison, and quickly—I'm late." I stepped on the gas and went straight there. A few minutes later, I was surprised to see a black airplane standing in the middle of a large field on the side of the by-road that *goes from Fresnes to Villejuif by way of L'Hay-les-Roses. At the same time, my client opened the separation-glass and shouted: "Stop!"*

" '*I took my foot off the gas, braked, declutched and stopped dead. The chap was already on the road. He threw me a 100-franc note and, without a word, started running across the field toward the airplane. At the same time, I heard the terrible racket of the motor. I was amazed, but I said to myself:* That was waiting for the Chinky; what's he up to? *I saw the man leap into the airplane, which immediately started moving over the field, and took off steeply at the far end. It gained height right away and went north.*

" '*I soon lost sight of it—but then, Monsieur, I heard loud bangs in the distance behind me. I got back on the road. Over there, where I knew the Saint-Clair house was, there were enormous clouds of black smoke.* Damn! *I said to myself.* There's been an explosion at the engineer's place. *And I drove off at 60 kilometers an hour,*[2] *like a madman, to warn the firemen in Fresnes, which was the closest station. Then, as I had a meeting with my boss at 10 a.m., and it was nearly 11, I came here—and here I am, ready to tell the whole story to a policeman like you....*' "

At this point Leo Saint-Clair interrupted his reading to turn the sheet over, for agent C88's report continued on the other side. Firmly, but with increasing excitement, he continued reading.

"*Such was the driver Motte's story. I interrogated him in order to get as complete and exact a description of the airplane as possible. Fortunately, the plane had*

---

[2] La Hire inserts a footnote here to observe that sixty kph was a very fast speed in 1912.

been close enough for him to get a good look at it during the two minutes that he had it before his eyes, and to make a mental note of numerous details of color, shape and construction.

"*When I got back to the Ministry I coordinated the information furnished to me by Monsieur Motte, and I am prepared to affirm, with certainty, that the suspect aircraft is a single-engine monoplane of the type known as a* Stagrad, *made in America and imported into Russia in parts for militarized assembly in the Dorf-Dasky workshops in the Posen region, on the German/Russian frontier.*

"*Conclusion: the* Stagrad *aircraft came from Russia, doubtless carrying the nihilist spy Sadi Khan, of whom our services lost sight five months ago. It would have landed unnoticed, having taken care to set down in open country far from any important agglomeration. It must have deposited the spy somewhere north of Paris yesterday evening, and came to pick him up this morning in the vicinity of the Saint-Clair house—which, moreover, has been the scene of a 'laboratory accident,' which it might perhaps be important to investigate, for the presence of the Russo-Mongol spy and revolutionary is suggestive of a premeditated crime.*

"*Signed: Agent C88.*"

Having finished reading this important report, Leo Saint-Clair looked at his three friends, who were sitting in an arc to his left, and said triumphantly: "Well, my friends, we're already on the track!"

As he took back the piece of paper and replaced it in to file, however, the Colonel shook his head, and said:

"A very vague track, Saint-Clair! Sadi Khan is a pseudonym of unknown origin. Furthermore, his face is similar to millions of Asiatic faces. Russia is vast, and

Asia is immense! A resident of Chicago, eh? It's not rare to find men of Chinese origin in America!"

"Well, Colonel," said Saint-Clair, "there's the scar on his forehead!"

"That's true," the officer conceded. "The criminal is marked by a recognizable sign. But let me tell you, my young friends, that the criminal isn't the most important thing in this terrible adventure—that's the invention, Radiant Z. Your duty to France, and your filial duty, my dear Leo, is primarily to recover the plants and models of the capto-projector, to get them back from the enemy, whoever that might be, and to bring them back to France. That's the most urgent thing."

"I know that perfectly well, Colonel," said Leo, sadly. "For, as Doctor Champeau has told you and hasn't concealed from me, it's by no means certain that my father will soon recover his full intelligence and the ability to work, by means of his brain-power, on the reconstitution and construction of Radiant Z. Our duty—my friends' and mine—is therefore to find and bring back the plans and the models before the enemy is able to study, understand and copy them. I know that a rather long and difficult preparatory study is necessary, even to make use of the models."

"Yes!" approved the officer, forcefully. "That's your duty, first and foremost. Besides, the discovery and punishment of the criminal might be achieved at the same time, God willing!"

"We shall pray that God wills it, Colonel!" And Leo Saint-Clair got up. His friends did likewise, as did Doctor Champeau and the officer.

"This evening," said the latter, "one of my agents will bring the documents I promised to you Bourg-la-Reine, and that agent will also bring you a great and useful surprise." He extended his hands and added, very emotionally: "Now, courage, intelligence and self-composure!" After kissing the four young men on both cheeks he embraced them paternally—and, hardened soldier though he was, he had tears in his eyes.

## Chapter IV: The First Adventure, The First Peril

That same evening—with the permission of their parents, who had been brought up to date by Doctor Champeau—René Croqui and Jean Degains, together with Robert Champeau, installed themselves for an overnight stay in the Saint-Clair house, in order to be in constant contact with their leader, Leo.

It was after dinner that they received the agent sent to them by the Colonel. The young man immediately made a good impression on the four friends—for he was indeed a young man, who looked even younger than he presumably was. He was short and slender, with an evident agility that did not exclude vigor, and had child-like bright blue eyes beneath his ruffled blond hair. If one studied those eyes closely, however, it was possible to divine that they were the focal points of a well-tempered soul. Received in the engineer's study, which the four friends had made into their conference-room, he introduced himself frankly and handed Leo Saint-Clair a square white envelope.

The leader opened he envelope and took out a piece of paper, which he unfolded, and over which he silently ran his eyes:

*My young friend.*

*This is to introduce my agent. His name is Wenceslas Polki, but we call him Polish Wen. His entire family was massacred in an outrage organized by Russian terrorists. In addition to his native tongue, he is fluent in French, Russian, English and German. He will be your interpreter, and will be precious. He is also a very well-*

*connected agent and a devoted servant. I have explained to him what this is about. Take him for the entire duration of your mission. You could not wish for a more useful and dependable companion He is 23 years old, but, although he is your elder, he will never forget that you are his commander and that your three comrades are your lieutenants.*

*To begin with, he is bringing you precious information that I have just received via the counter-espionage brigade of the Sûreté Générale of the Eastern region.*

*Courage and good luck, my friends!*

And the Colonel had signed it, underlining his illustrious name with a vigorous flourish.

Leo Saint-Clair passed the letter to his comrades, who were grouped behind him. "Read it," he said. Then he went to Wen, who had stepped back discreetly, and offered him his hand, smiling amicably. "Be welcome among us, Wen," he said. "The Colonel's letter and your appearance suffice for us to see you from now on as a comrade, determined to brave the same perils and enjoy the same success as the four of us."

Wenceslas Polki blushed with pleasure and pride. He shook the proffered hand, and, with as much dignity as modesty, replied in a firm and very warm voice: "Thank you, Monsieur Saint-Clair. As the Colonel must have told you, you can count on me. To you and your friends, though, I shall be an interpreter, a guide, a liaison officer and an orderly—in brief, a soldier! How should I address you?"

Leo smiled, and simply said: "My fellow rugby-players call me Chief."

"Understood, Chief!" said Wen, standing to attention.

"As for my comrades," Leo continued, still smiling, "I'm sure that they share my opinion regarding your reciprocal relationship. I'll name them as I point them out to you: Robert Champeau, René Croqui, Jean Degains. You can call them by their first names, affectionately, and they'll call you Wen, with cordial familiarity."

"I beg your pardon," said René Croqui, coming forward and offering his hand to the Pole, "but there's one thing the Chief forgot to mention. As you can see, I'm the joker of the party. It's my nature, and that's why I'm nicknamed Croquignol. When you're in a bad mood, my dear Wen, you can call me Croquignol. That will cheer you up." And René Croqui broke into a smile. His good humor was, as always, contagious. Leo Saint-Clair laughed. Champeau and Degains laughed too, and Wen could not help doing likewise.

Thus the pact of solidarity was joyously concluded.

Immediately becoming serious again, though—for the circumstances were grave—the Chief said: "When you arrived, Wen, we were about to form a sort of Council of War, to take decisions regarding practical action. Let's sit down. The session is open. First, it's up to you to communicate the precious information that the colonel's letter mentions."

While speaking, Leo had indicated several chairs with his hand. Each of them took one. The four Frenchmen and the Pole sat down around the square table that stood in the middle of the room beneath an electric ceiling-light. There was a big atlas on the table, along with several road-maps, blank paper and propelling pencils.

All gazes turned to Wen's face, and the Pole spoke unhesitatingly. "The information can be conveyed in a few words. The *Stagrad* airplane, which took off from the field bordering the Fresnes road, didn't get as far as its occupants undoubtedly wished. A storm wind probably constrained it to set an eastward course, and a mechanical breakdown obliged it to set down in the Doubs valley, in a meadow near Montbéliard. A detachment of gendarmes is surrounding it but the aviators have disappeared. The colonel and the Sûreté Générale immediately telegraphed orders for the region's railway stations and the Swiss frontier to be discreetly but closely watched—for it's important that the operation be kept secret.

"The Colonel thinks that you, Chief, will doubtless want to get moving immediately and try to capture Sadi Khan before he can reach Germany—which is still possible for a clever and experienced man, in spite of all organized surveillance."

"My God!" exclaimed Saint-Clair, getting to his feet. "If that's the case, there's no time to lose! Minutes are precious. Let's go!"

That morning, after leaving the Ministry of War, Leo Saint-Clair had laid out the first considerable expense attributed to the mission's budget. For years—even though he was not yet 21—he had been an automobile fanatic. Benefiting from an official exemption, he had already had a driving license for five years. He had passed successively from a little five-horsepower engine to the valve-less 18-horsepower engine that animated his present vehicle, the red cabriolet. Ever since the last Motor Show, however, he had dreamed of trying out a 40-horsepower five-seater sports car, with steel-grey bodywork, one of which was on show and on sale—already run in and ready to take to the road without delay—in a large garage on the Avenue Malakoff. And that very morning, Leo Saint-Clair had bought what he called "my Forty." It had been delivered to him at about 3 p.m., and was presently in a garage situated in the Saint-Clair commons, completely kitted out, with its tanks full.

Having kissed the forehead of his sleeping father, and fervently embraced his mother—who was in tears, but fully determined to encourage her son and give him her approval—Leo rejoined his four companions, who had run to the garage following his "Let's go!" They had been ready for an abrupt departure for hours.

Helmeted, gauntleted and wrapped up tightly, Leo installed himself at the Forty's steering-wheel. Beside him was Jean Degains, a seasoned mechanic, whose hands were as skillful as his mind was adept. Robert Champeau, René Croqui, alias Croquignol, and Wenceslas Polki, alias Wen, sat side by side on the deep and broad padded rear seat.

With all the headlights on, the steel-grey roadster emerged from the garage, went through the grounds, and through the gate opened by Antoine. Once on the road it sped away, purring softly, rapidly cutting through the wind in the direction of the Croix-de-Berny. There it turned left, quickly reached Choisy-le-Roi and the crossroads at Bonneuil, and then went through Boissy-Saint Léger, Brie-Comte-Robert, Guignes-Rabutin, Nangis and Provins, eventually attaining a record speed—between 90 and 100 kilometers an hour—on the highway from Paris to Belfort, via Troyes, Chaumont and Langres.

At Belfort, the young driver went around the town and sped southwards toward Montbéliard.

When the Forty entered the little town, the kilometric indicator, set at zero at the point of departure, displayed the number 425, and the chronometer marked 3 a.m—in the morning on Thursday March 5, 1912. They had left Bourg-la-Reine at 9 p.m. the previous evening.

They had, therefore, covered 425 kilometers in six nocturnal hours, at a mean speed of 70 kph.

The main square of Montbéliard, very picturesque and original in character, is partly bordered on one side by the ancient church of Saint-Martin, now Protestant. It is a beautiful 16th century edifice, the durability of whose interior architecture—especially its ceiling—is much vaunted. It was in front of this building that Leon Saint-Clair brought the sports car to a halt.

At 3 a.m., however, and in the present circumstances, that halt was not motivated by the picturesque architecture of the ancient church. The friends and the Pole gave no thought to contemplating either façade, which were, in any case, plunged in a darkness that the humble street-lights of the square could not succeed in dispelling. If they were stopping there, it was because someone as waiting for them there. The four young people knew that, Wen having specified that the Colonel had talked on the telephone to the Prefect of Doubs, and that the Prefect had taken care to alert the Adjutant in command of the Montbéliard gendarmerie, that small town being the nearest one to the fallow field in which the black airplane had made a forced landing.

On the threshold of what would undoubtedly be many very exciting adventures, into which the four young Frenchmen and their Polish companions were now launched, it is important for us to have better descriptions of the physical and moral character of these brave lads.

Leo Saint-Clair, the Chief, was a tall, handsome fellow with black hair, eyes the color of roasted hazelnuts, and well-defined features that were both delicate and energetic. He was a complete athlete, at least to the extent that his youth permitted. He had a very quick and lively intelligence, a commanding and decisive gaze, indomitable will-power, as much wise prudence as heroic courage, and, to cap it all, a heart of gold. His voice was firm and sonorous, incisive and very virile, clearly authoritative in certain circumstances but soft and jovial when it was time for smiles and serenity. He exercised great prestige over his comrades, by virtue of his personal qualities and the manner in which he carried out the functions of captain at rugby.

Robert Champeau was rather short, but stocky and thick-set, with a truly exceptional physical strength. Even so, he had considerable manual dexterity, due to the fact that his father had not only made him a nurse of the first order but also a medical and surgical assistant capable, in pressing circumstances, of administering the initial—and often most vital—cares of medicine and surgery. He had bright chestnut-colored hair, grey-blue eyes, and a somewhat angular face, slightly coarse and bad-tempered in appearance, although he too had a very good heart. His voice was a little hoarse, and usually soft and discreet. He was courageous, of course, with a Breton stubbornness that became an invincible obstinacy in grave circumstances. He was bound to Leo Saint-Clair by an affection that dated from their earliest steps, and which was genuinely fraternal.

René Croqui was of medium height, but he seemed taller because he was thin, gangling and given to gesticulation. Lightly blond, with sparkling black eyes, and a bony oval face, he seemed serious because he habitually maintained a malicious reserve; let off the leash, however, he was a Parisian street-urchin with a mocking voice, a punning, joking hooligan with an inexhaustibly fertile comic imagination. People call him Croquignole, which they pronounced Croquignol![3] He was brave and valiant, but in the most bizarre fashion—which is to say, with the appearances of the most astonishing fearfulness. The fallacious excess of that fearfulness launched him, doubtless by compensation, into the craziest temerities. "Oh, that Croquignol's a character!" they said of him in the society of young football fans. Yes he was, and no ordinary character.

As for Jean Degains, he was of indeterminate height, normal corpulence and medium strength, but possessed of marvelous suppleness, agility and dexterity. He had reddish hair, with bright green eyes specked with gold, a long face, and very white skin with a few russet blotches. He joked about himself and did justice to himself at the same time in saying, in a clear and tranquil tone: "I might be carrot-topped but I'm not bone idle."[4] Indeed, no one was quicker than him in coming forward. His mechanical ingenuity, in construction and making repairs, was prodigious, served by a manual skill that continually pushed back the limits of the possible. He was capable of patching up a motor with materials drawn from a sardine tin and opening the most complicated locks with a piece of wire. He had all the courage he needed, but he was cunning above all, either spontaneously and impulsively, or reflectively, calculatedly

---

[3] A *croquignole* is a small, crisp pastry or a flick of the finger administered to the nose. The noun is feminine, but its masculinization as Croquignol creates a kinship with guignol, a term applied to a grotesque glove-puppet akin to the English Punch (as in the Grand-Guignol theater).
[4] What Degains actually says is "Possible que je sois *Poil-de-carotte*, mais je ne suis pas *Poil-dans-la-main*!" The wordplay is untranslatable.

and very knowledgeably, according to the circumstances.

That was our quartet.

As for their companion and auxiliary, Wenceslas Polki, we have already described him as aged 23, but not looking any older than 20, and apt to give himself an art of being even younger. He was small, slender, agile and strong all that the same time, with disheveled blond hair. He had bright blue eyes set in a thin and quite child-like face—and he possessed a well-tempered soul.

Such were the five bold fellows who, in the pitch dark of the early hours of Thursday March 5, 1912, leapt out of the steel-grey roadster on to the rounded pavement of the main square of Montbéliard.

Let us add that Saint-Clair, Champeau, Croqui and Degains were dressed in their everyday clothes, with fur-lined leather overcoats; that Wen was wearing a golfing costume with a long, very warm cloak of thick but light cloth; that all of them had fur hats with ear-flaps and thick gloves. And let us note that on leaving the family home, Leo Saint-Clair had said: "We'll buy clothes and underwear, and whatever else we need, on the way."

Of the five young men, only Wen Polki was armed; at his waist, on the right, a little above and behind the fly of his trousers, he had a solidly-mounted leather holster, which contained a Browning loaded with seven bullets.

As soon as they were out of the car, Leo Sant-Clair ordered: "Champeau, Croqui, Degains, stay here and guard the car. Wen, come with me." And he set off along a corridor leading to the office of the gendarmerie. A door had already opened, inscribing a rectangle of light on the somber façade of the edifice.

"Come in, gentlemen," said a cordial voice with a strong Alsatian accent. "As you can see, you're expected." This was Adjutant Mutz, the Commander of the Montbéliard gendarmerie. He did not ask his visitors to sit down when they had shaken his hand. Having closed the door again, he immediately said to the first man to enter: "It's Monsieur Leo Saint-Clair, isn't it? Good. Your rooms are ready at the Hôtel du Vieux-Chaudron. You can get a few hours rest. Tomorrow, I think, you'll be leaving for Switzerland."

"For Switzerland?" Leo echoed, in surprise.

"Yes. This is what I've been instructed to tell you, summarizing all the information received since yesterday which is in accord with certain older items of information of which you'll have the benefit." He took a deep breath, for he was fat and a trifle asthmatic, then continued: "It's possible that the black airplane had fled before the north-westerly storm, but having headed north after taking off from Bourg-la-Reine it would have headed east anyway, and then south-east, because it was to Switzerland that Sadi Khan had to go. An engine-breakdown forced the black airplane to land near Montbéliard instead of setting down close to Basle, not far from the Swiss frontier, where accomplices were waiting for it. We know that, and we also know that Sadi Khan and the pilot of the black airplane have taken the train at Belford for Basle. And finally, we know that on the shore of Lake Geneva—*on the shore*, you understand, *near the water's edge?*—in a property whose exact location is unfortunately unknown to us, international, or rather Russo-Asiatic spies, certainly nihilists, have installed their general headquarters. That's where Sadi Khan and his companion are headed."

"Then that's where we're going!" exclaimed Saint-Clair.

"Of course!" said the Adjutant. "Listen to me. For diplomatic reasons, the French and Swiss police are maintaining the greatest caution in this affair, effectively remaining inactive, but you can act. You can go to Switzerland as simple tourists. Your passports are on that table. They bear your true forenames, but they give each of you a false family name. It's possible that a Saint-Clair and a Champeau might alert the enemy, but your forenames haven't been changed, so that you can address one another with all the ease associated with habitual names. Understood? Good! You'll have *carte blanche* over here. Are you armed?"

"No," Saint-Clair replied, intensely interested.

"That's been anticipated. Look over here. These little Brownings in holsters are for you. It's necessary to conceal the weapons in the right-hand pockets of your trousers, so that they'll be invisible but within easy reach. I warn you—you'll have to make use of them! Bah! God is with you, since you're going up against Sa-di Khan. I won't keep you any longer. You need to rest, and sleep until for least five hours. No one's any good after a sleepless night." Accompanying his words with prompt gestures, the adjutant concluded: "Here are the passports, and here are the Brownings. Take them all, Wen. You can divide them up in the car. Ah! The Hôtel du Vieux-Chaudron is at the end of the first street on the left. Comfortable rooms and good beds await you there. Just past the porch there's a garage that communicates with the interior of the hotel. The night-clerk will open up to you at the first sound of the horn. *Adieu*, Monsieur Saint-Clair. *Au revoir*, Wen. And good luck!"

The entire scene had lasted less than five minutes.

"Well," said Leo to his companions before getting back into the car, "Adjutant Mutz doesn't beat around the bush. He was rapid, precise and clear. I'll explain everything to you at the hotel."

At the hotel, after the explanations, which Champeau, Croqui and Degains greeted with enthusiasm, the four young men and the Pole went to bed. It was now 3:45 a.m. They slept until 9 a.m. At 10 a.m., furnished with their passports, armed and vibrant with hope, they were on their way again.

On March 5, the weather in the region was fine, cold and dry, with a clear sky and a north wind. The steel-grey sports car sped along the well-maintained road with the wind behind it, at great speed and noiselessly, though Belfort, Delle and across the Franco-Swiss border. The formalities of passing through customs were brief, the passports and the auto-triptych given to them by Adjutant Mutz were perfectly in order.

They could only travel at moderate speed on the steep and difficult road from Delle to Délémont, where they ate a late lunch; then they went on to Neuchâtel, traveling along the side of the lake, turning toward Lausanne at Yverdon.

"Finally, we can get on work," Leo Saint-Clair announced, gravely.

Wen, who knew Lausanne, pointed out a good second-rate hotel equipped with a garage with closed door. It was the Hôtel du Pélican.

The four Frenchmen and the Pole took baths there, ate dinner and went to bed, wisely putting off to the next day their first personal investigations of the trail of the Z Projector and its criminal possessor.

The young men had chosen three rooms with communicating doors, two of them with two beds and the third with only one. The bore the numbers 15, 16 and 17.

Leo Saint-Clair and Robert Champeau installed themselves in the first, René Croqui and Jean Degains in the second, and Wenceslas Polki in the third, number 17. Each of the three rooms was equipped with a W.C., but in forming a distinct apartment they only had one bathroom. They were arranged in a straight line, with three third-floor windows on the façade, with a southward view over the wide and beautiful Avenue de la Gare. Their doors, and that of the bathroom, opened on to a corridor, at the far end, as far away as possible from the head of the staircase. They were not very large, but were ingeniously arranged, neat and comfortable; they would have lent themselves to a longer stay.

On the morning of March 6, Wen was the first to wake up. The two interior doors communicating with the other two rooms had remained open all night. Sufficient dawn light came in through the gap in the casements and shutters, which had been left hygienically ajar, so that the Pole would be able to see what time it was on his watch, placed on the bedside table.

"Quarter past six!" Wen muttered. "All right. Are they asleep? Yes, probably. One of them is snoring. I'll get up. I'll follow up the idea that I had last night. If I succeed, the terrains will be considerably cleared, and I'll have more chance of a swift enlightenment...and may I be hanged if we aren't hot on the trail in less than 24 hours."

He slid out of bed and went on tiptoe to close the door to the next room, where Croqui and Degains were sleeping like babes. After having opened the shutters wide and closed the casements of his window, he washed rapidly and dressed himself from top to toe. Then he took out a pencil and wrote on his notepad:

*Don't worry about me. I've gone out. If I'm not back by noon, have lunch without me—but afterwards, I beg you to wait for me here, for I'll need to talk to you as soon as I get back. W.*

He tore off the sheet and attached it to the pillow on his bed with a pin, directly under the beam of the bedside light, which he switched on-and he went out, carefully closing and locking the door to the corridor. He took the key with him.

The first person to see the piece of paper on the pillow was Jean Degains. Having woken up at 7 a.m., he had chatted briefly with René Croqui, who had also just opened his eyes. They had heard the attenuated voice of Saint-Clair coming from room 15: "Hey! Good morning, friends! Is everyone awake?"

"Here, yes," Croqui had replied.

"Here too, and good morning!" said Robert Champeau, stretching.

"Oh!" said Degains. "Comrade Wen has closed his door?" He leapt out of bed in his pajamas, bare-footed, went straight to the closed door and opened it. Immediately, he saw the lighted lamp, the empty bed and the pinned sheet of paper. "Oh! Right…he's gone out!" he muttered. And, accompanied by René, who had got out of bed, Jean went to take the note to the Chief.

In Room 15, Saint-Clair and Champeau, who were out of bed, were in the process of opening the shutters and closing the windows. A horizontal and oblique sunbeam was gilding the panes, and it was by that joyous light that the four friends, bringing their heads together, read Wen's note.

"Very good!" said Saint-Clair. "He knows Lausanne well. He has an idea."

"But what about us? What shall we do this morning?"

"Well, we're tourists. What do tourists do on the first day? They look around. We'll simply take the car and go half way around Lake Geneva—and as we have a secret agenda, we'll take any opportunity to chat to the people we meet, look carefully at slightly isolated private houses...slightly isolated, while being quite close to the water's edge..."

"Right!" groaned Champeau. "Good idea—but let's not waste time. I'll die of hunger, Leo, if we don't order breakfast immediately."

"Order away!"

Robert rang. The friends separated in order to wash and dress.

Two waitresses brought four servings of bread rolls and hot chocolate. They ate with hearty appetites.

At 8 a.m., they brought the steel-grey roadster out of its box. The courtyard of the communal garage and the private boxes was to the west of the Hôtel du Pélican, separated from the Avenue de la Gare by a high wall and communicating with that avenue by means of a large gate with two wooden battens that moved to the left and right on rollers fitted to iron rails.

The four friends' automobile made a sensational exit from this gate; the Touring Club's triangular flag in the French colors floated from a staff to the left of the windscreen, and the steel-grey sports car, with its long hood, under which the 40 horse-power engine thrummed and roared, had everything needed to attract all gazes, excite curiosity and provoke admiration.

All of that, a trifle ostentatious, was intentional—for, following the lead of the cunning Degains, they had reasoned as follows: "Let's not seem to be hiding. On the contrary, let's make a show of being what we want people to think we are: French sportsmen on a tourist trip by car and on foot. As the names on our passports— the only names by which anyone here know us—can't give us away, no one will imagine that young men so expansive in every way are really secret detectives on a counter-espionage mission. Thus, the more we show off, the better masked we shall really be, free to act without provoking the suspicion of anyone we might encounter by chance who has reasons for mistrusting any new face."

Leaving the Avenue de la Gare at the first junction to the left, Leo took the automobile along the road to Ouchy, and then headed westwards—which is to say, in the direction of Geneva—on the highway along the shore of the lake.

It is only 61 kilometers from Lausanne to Geneva but, rolling along at a moderate speed, after the fashion of tourists who do not want to miss any of the country-side, often stopping at sites or viewpoints that were par-ticularly picturesque, the steel-grey roadster took an hour and a half to cover that distance.

As they came into Geneva, Saint-Clair turned round, for there was nothing they wanted to see in the town. Then he stopped, in a spot without too many hous-es nearby, to exchange a few words with his friends.

"Nothing suspect!" he said to Champeau.

"Nothing," said Robert.

They both turned round in order to talk to their comrades over the rear windscreen. "Well?" asked the Chief.

Croqui and Desgains replied together: "Nothing seen"—but the latter added: "The house in question might have a perfectly innocent appearance, you know.

It isn't some more-or-less remarkable villa that I'd suspect, but rather one that won't attract any attention in its isolation, and might even be hidden behind a curtain of trees of some sort…"

"We'll go back to Lausanne, then," Saint-Clair concluded. "But let's come to an agreement. I'll keep my attention focused on the car. Robert will inspect the right-hand side of the road—the lake side, which has fewer houses. And you two, Jean and René, will observe the left-hand side, the hills. As we came out, we had general views that permitted us to eliminate a priori those villas that are too conspicuous or too luxurious; as we return, our attention should pick up certain details that might have escaped us."

"Fine!"

"Understood!"

"*All right!*" exclaimed Degains, in English—which he spoke rather well, and whose most current expressions he liked to employ.

And the automobile moved off.

Three quarters of an hour later, and 35 kilometers further on, the first significant incident of the great adventure occurred—a most unexpected incident, which immediately made the four boys think: "This time, we're off!"

They had just come through the little town of Rolle and had reached the flat promontory traversed by the river Aubonne when a shout rang out in the pure and clear air: "Help!"—a vibrant cry that made Saint-Clair come to a halt in the space of three meters.

"That's Wen's voice!" said Croqui, excitedly.

Immediately, the voice repeated: "Help! Help!… He…lp!" Thus time, it was weaker, and the third repetition was choked off.

"Oh!" exclaimed Degains. "It came from behind that wall!"

To the right, masking the view of the lake, there was a curtain of large poplars clustered behind a white wall about two meters high. There was no opening along the entire length of the wall, but Champeau had noticed, unthinkingly, that a little by-road bordered by willows branched off from the main road at the corner of the wall, ending into large iron gate breaking the line of the wall at right-angles to the highway. Rapidly, he gave that information to the Chief.

"Bah!" said Saint-Clair. "Better to go over the wall—that'll be quicker!" And he instructed, in a soft but imperious voice: "Out of the car! René, come and make a ladder for us, then stay and guard the car. If necessary, defend it with armed force!"

They were first-rate gymnasts. Hearts beating rapidly, but with their minds clear and their courage taut, they did what needed to be done. René Croqui braced himself, set his back to the wall and joined his hands into a supple but solid stirrup in front of his belly. Putting one foot there, the other on his shoulder and his hands on the crest of the wall, Leo Saint-Clair was the first to go up and leap down on the other side. Robert Champeau and Jean Degains followed him at one-second intervals.

Inside the vast enclosure, the trunks of the poplars were lined up two meters from the wall. Passing between them, the three young men ran straight ahead across an unkempt lawn toward an open pathway between trees of various species, at the far end of which the white walls of a house could be seen, their whiteness contrasting with the black rectangles of two windows.

They heard no more cries, nor did they see anyone or perceive any sound of flight. Moving with one accord, however, Leo, Robert and Jean went all the way to the house as if to go in like a whirlwind, for one of the visible windows was wide open. As they ran across the lawn and along the excessively sandy path, however, they had such a violent impression of isolation, solitude and impending ambush that Saint-Clair, expressing his own and his companions' profoundest thought, ordered in a dull voice: "Brownings at the ready!"

He drew his weapon; Champeau and Degains did likewise—without relenting in their rapid pace.

Their minds were working hard, though. Saint-Clair's was prudent, Degains' was cunning and Champeau's was opposed to any feverish haste. The first impulse had launched all three of them over the wall behind which Wenceslas' voice had called for help, and, as a logical consequence, had hurled them toward the house that appeared at the end of the wooded path beyond the empty lawn—but the mental trajectory of that impulse had reached its terminus. At the same time, their material course slowed down and stopped dead at the moment when the three runners were on the point of emerging from the shady pathway into the bright light of the narrow pebble-strewn esplanade circling the house.

"Stop!" breathed the Chief.

"Yes," said Champeau.

"Right!" approved Degains.

And with the same movement they took cover, side by side, behind one of the enormous spindle-tree bushes that bordered the esplanade at intervals, facing the house on the edge of the little wood.

With a brief smile, Leo Saint-Clair murmured; "That was a very good charge...but we risk throwing ourselves into the wolf's jaws."

"We don't know how many men there are in the house," Robert Champeau muttered, softly. "And we know that they don't hesitate to use violence, for if Wen hadn't been attacked he wouldn't have called for help. An instinctive cry, of course! He didn't know that Providence had determined that we'd be passing along the road within the range of his voice. By force of numbers and determined violence, the occupants of the house would have killed or captured us...and our mission would have been all over, pitifully!"

"Right!" said Degains. He did not add another word—but through the gaps in the bush his keen eyes were observing the house, and his ears, endowed with a great delicacy and a rare acuity, were listening...

Leo and Robert knew Cunning Jean well. They looked at him, and they waited, knowing that an idea was about to hatch in his ingenious brain—a good idea, which the Chief's superior intelligence could not help but welcome and adapt to the circumstances for its execution.

Jean Degains' silent observation and reflection, and his comrades' anticipation, lasted no more than a minute. Suddenly, the Briard ceased studying the flat façade of the house with its eight windows, two of which were open, and its little perron surmounted by a closed door. After a brief glance at Champeau—who was frowning, as usual—he fixed his eyes on the gravely attentive face of Leo Saint-Clair, the Chief, and said, in a low voice: "I can hear someone talking inside the house, in a language I don't understand. There are two voices; one's asking questions at length, the other's making monosyllabic replies that seemed to me to be obstinate negations. So, my idea is to get closer, even to enter the house through one of the open windows—the window of the room that isn't the one in which the people are talking."

"Are you sure that one of the two rooms is unoccupied?" Saint-Clair asked.

"Quite certain!" Degains replied, firmly. "The people who are talking are in the other room with the open window. It's a hundred to one that, if there are more than two people there—which is probable, for Wen wouldn't have been beaten down by one lone man, all those individuals are assembled in the room where the talking is going on, where the Pole is being subjected, if I'm not mistaken, to an interrogation."

Leo was convinced and, as always, was led to give Degains the permission for which he was courageously asking. "Well then, go!" he said. "But be careful! If you're in danger, fire a shot. We'll come running."

Jean smiled thinly and murmured; "You know perfectly well, Chief, that there's no need to tell Cunning Jean to be careful!"

With his Browning in his hand, he went around the bush, bent down, and rapidly passed over the esplanade, taking care not to step on the pebbles, where his tread would have produced a disastrous sound, but using a sort of cement walkway as broad as the perron, which led from the end of the path to the door. There he turned left and inched along the wall to the first open window, which he had indicated with a gesture as being that of the room in which no one was talking.

It is easy to imagine how passionately interested Leo Saint-Clair and Robert Champeau were, behind the bush that hid them completely while permitting them to see quite well, and how fast their hearts were beating as they waited attentively.

Jean Degains came to a stop beneath the window, bent double, and slowly straightened up, leaning slightly to one side so that as little as possible of his head would show in the window-frame. At first, he only darted a glance into the room from low down on the right-hand side of the window. At the same time, he lifted his gun hand, holding it in a convenient position for aiming and firing, in case any danger surged forth so great that taking the offensive as the only means of avoiding it.

Suddenly, he froze again—although he was not confronted by any immediate peril, since he lowered his weapon and his head remained in a position such that his left eye could see into the room.

That immobility only lasted a few seconds. Then Degains carefully holstered his Browing, took hold of the window-sill with both hands, braced himself with his elbows and his knees, and flexed his body, raising himself up to sit on the widow-ledge, over which he immediately slid, until his feet were doubtless touching the floor inside.

Saint-Clair and Champeau saw him vanish entirely into the room, whose depths were dark, there being no other window to light it from the far side. The Chief and his friend had no time to wonder about their comrade's entry into the house, though, for an instant after his disappearance, they heard and recognized his voice, shouting: "Hands up! Hands up!"

"Churka!" yelped a strange shrill voice—and there was a loud bang, immediately followed by a thunderous racket, like a door being slammed on the run, with brutal violence.

Saint-Clair and Champeau lost no time in reflection or deliberation.

"Hup!" exclaimed Leo.

"Yes!" said Robert.

And they leapt forward. The noise they made running over the pebbles hardly mattered now. The two lads took the shortest route, straight toward the second window—the one on the left, the one to the room in which Degains had cried out. They reached it at the same time. Together, side by side, they hoisted themselves up and leapt in—and stopped dead.

Jean Degains was kneeling in front of them, next to an overturned table, his Browning on the carpet beside him. On that same carpet, Wenceslas Polki was lying on his back—and Degains' agile fingers were working to free the Pole from a finely-woven cord tightened about his neck.

Jean did not turn his head at his comrades' abrupt entrance, which he had anticipated, but he said, in a voice breathless with emotion: "The villains! One of them fired at me. The other tightened this cord, whose slip-knot was passed around Wen's neck—pulled it so brutally that the cord has cut into the skin. Look—it's bleeding!"

"Wait!" said Champeau.

He bent down, put his ear to Wen's chest, listened for a few seconds, straightened up again, and looked at Saint-Clair and Degains, who were standing at the Pole's feet, very perplexed. Rapidly, he said: "Don't worry. He's only lost consciousness—more from the pain of the tightening than lack of breath; the strangulation didn't last long enough for him to be asphyxiated."

"What about the bandits?" Saint-Clair asked.

"Two!" Degains replied. "Ran out by the back door."

"Let's go after them, Jean," said the Chief, decisively. "Robert, you can look after Wen."

49

"Of course," Champeau murmured.

The door at the back of the room led to a corridor, with another facing door; then there was a large room furnished as a dining-room, which communicated with an almost treeless flower-garden by means of a wide open set of French windows. At the back of the garden, beyond a low wall surmounted by decorative railings, the waters of Lake Geneva extended, very blue beneath the clear sky, all the way to the distant French shore, where a high mountain loomed over Thonon.

As they ran across the garden toward a small gate in the wall that was still open, however, the two *forwards* [5] heard the sputtering racket of a powerful engine. As they came through the gate, they saw a white motor-boat, whose propeller was making an enormous wake. It had undoubtedly just cast off from the little jetty that was there. It was speeding away. There were two men in it, one standing in the middle, the other seated at the rear. Leo and Jean could only see their backs.

"Too late!" said Saint-Clair.

"That's unlucky," groaned Degains.

They were tempted to fire at the two fleeing men, but their wise intelligence resisted the temptation. The distance was already considerable. There are very few sharpshooters sufficiently experienced to hit a target— even a large one—with a Browning at more than 50 meters, and the two "forwards," needless to say, were not very experienced. In any case, two fishing-boats were

---

[5] The reference is presumably to rugby positions, although only one of the four friends (Champeau) seems to be built for the scrum and he is not present at this point; the designation is, however, used again on other occasions with no more obvious propriety.

close at hand, and, not far away from the fleeing motor-boat, a pleasure yacht was sailing, driven by the fresh breeze of that fine March day. Gunshots, therefore, even if they had no direct effect, risked causing indirect complications that it was important to avoid, since secrecy had to be maintained with respect to their present mission.

"Let's go back," Saint-Clair decided. "Wen must have something interesting to tell us."

They went back—which is to say that they went through the garden, the dining-room and the wide corridor. Degains opened the door of the room in which they had left Chapeau to look after Wen.

"Uh-oh!" he exclaimed.

"My God!" said Saint-Clair.

They saw Champeau seated on the carpet; his eyes were wild and his hesitant hands were feeling his skull.

"I've been attacked," he stammered, as he recognized his two comrades. "Three men—a truncheon-blow to my head. They've taken Wen."

At the same moment, though, a loud scream resounded outside: "Aah!" It was followed by a cry for help: the old rallying cry of the Lion Cub scout-troop, to which Degains, Champeau and Croqui had all belonged: "Rahioooh!"

"My God!" exclaimed Saint-Clair. "Croquignol! He's under attack!"

He jumped out of the window with a single bound, and ran forward. Having leapt out after him, Degains was hot on his heels. Within three seconds, with prodigious skill and speed, lifting and hoisting one another up, they climbed over the wall behind the screen of poplars. Champeau had got to his feet and followed some way behind.

In the ditch at the foot of the wall, outside, they saw Croqui getting to his feet, and heard him say to them, breathlessly: "One of the three is a first-rate boxer. They came from the corner of the wall, over there. I didn't see them until they were on top of me. Two of them were carrying Wen, who seemed to be dead. The other, who came on ahead, ran at me—that as when I shouted. I tried to fire my Browning, but a blow from a fist knocked it out of my hand, and another punch in the chest knocked me into the ditch. They've taken the car..."

On the highway, heading toward Lausanne, the steel-grey sports car was shrinking into the distance, moving very rapidly—carrying three mysterious spies along with the unfortunate Polki.

Suddenly, a puff of white smoke spread out above and behind the automobile, and a muffled detonation sounded in the blue air.

Leo Saint-Clair staggered, collapsed and fell—and his horrified companions saw that his face was entirely bathed in blood...

## Chapter V: The Birth of the Nyctalope

That an armed combat could take place in broad daylight, on the edge of a busy road, on the shore of a lake where yachts are passing and small boats peacefully carrying fishermen, says a great deal about the impudent audacity and the decisive intent of the mysterious gang whose leader was undoubtedly the enigmatic spy Sadi Khan, alias Theodore Wallis of Chicago.

It is not uncommon, however, for young sportsmen to practice rifle-shooting in the gardens of villas, and a few gunshots were not likely to astonish the fishermen and yachtsmen. The skirmish, partly masked and muffled in any case by the house, the walls and the trees in the garden, thus passed unnoticed. If anyone saw the puff of smoke behind the grey car speeding toward Lausanne, they must have taken it for a normal product of the exhaust-pipe.

The result was that, for several minutes, there was no one but Champeau, Croqui and Degains gathered around the prostrate Saint-Clair, who was lying beside the ditch that ran along the road, near a little bridge giving access to a service-gate etched in the long wall of the tragic villa. The punches received by the second and the truncheon-blow received by the first were not serious, and for the moment, Champeau, like the good surgeon's son he was, was entirely focused on Saint-Clair's wound.

"Calm down!" he ordered his two comrades. "It's only a superficial wound. Leo's only fainted. Without touching the eye, the bullet has struck the corner of the orbit and grazed the temporal bone on the right hand side, as you can see. The best thing to do is to carry the Chief into the villa, since we no longer have our automobile. I noticed that there's a telephone in the room where we found Polki initially, half-strangled. We'll summon a doctor from Lausanne."

"Yes," said Degains.

"Wait!" said Croqui. "Here comes a car!"

Approaching noiselessly from the direction of Geneva, a large and handsome limousine came to a halt. Evidently, the chauffeur and the footman had noticed the singular group of three young men leaning over a fourth, who was lying on the road, from some distance away. Perhaps the footman had related that incident to the people inside the vehicle. At any rate, a door opened and an old gentleman and a young woman got out of the limousine and came over, asking what had happened.

Circumspectly, Champeau replied: "An accident. We were about to go into that villa and telephone Lausanne to ask for a doctor…"

But the gentleman, whose face, framed with short-cropped and wispy white hair, had an energetic and benevolent air about it, said: "Are you French, Messieurs?"

"Yes, Monsieur," Champeau replied.

"So am I—and its Providence that brought me here, judiciously. I'm staying in Lausanne—where my brother-in-law, Doctor de Villiers-Pagan, has a medical practice—until May. The interior of my limousine has six seats. I'd be happy to take all three of you, and your injured friend. We can deposit him, if you wish, at my brother-in-law's clinic. I'm retired General Le Breuil, of Tours, and this is Mademoiselle Aurora Malianova, a nurse in the Villiers-Pagan clinic." He gestured toward the young woman who had climbed out of the limousine after him: a very serious and very beautiful blue-eyed blonde.

The best thing was to accept. Champeau did not hesitate; he saw at a glance that Croqui and Degains were in agreement. He pronounced the appropriate words of acquiescence and gratitude.

In the depths of their being, however, the three young men—still very young and so poorly armed against the vicissitudes of life—felt crippled by this first blow, which was, in truth, very heavy. Before they arrived in Lausanne, Robert Champeau, inspired by the confidence of inexperience, but after having demanded nevertheless a formal promise of absolute discretion, had confided in General Le Breil all the essentials of their dramatic adventure.

"*Fichtre!*" muttered the General, excited and admiring—and he looked more closely at Leo Saint-Clair, who, wedged between Croqui and Degains, had had his forehead bathed with ether and summarily bandaged by Mademoiselle Aurora Malianova, thanks to the resources of a small portable first-aid kit that was always stowed away in an interior corner of the limousine. No one noticed the strange hardness of the gaze that the young woman fixed upon Saint-Clair.

Leo was still unconscious, but the regular beat of his pulse and his normal respiration clearly indicated that, save for any consequences of nervous trauma, his general health was as well as could be expected. That condition was not modified in the slightest until he was installed in the only bed in a room in a clinic in the Rue du Petit-Chêne in Lausanne, where Leo Saint-Clair received the attentions of Doctor de Villiers-Pagan. Mademoiselle Aurora, who had rapidly donned her nurse's uniform, served as his assistant. At the back of the room, standing to either side of General Le Breuil, Champeau, Croqui and Degains waited very anxiously, fearful and confident at the same time.

First the surgeon unbandaged the wound, had it carefully washed by Aurora, and examined it closely.

"There won't be any lasting damage," he said. "Only a minuscule scar will remain visible at close range—but the handsome lad's had a lucky escape!"

The wound was sterilized and the dressing replaced. Then Monsieur de Villiers-Pagan administered an intravenous injection in the left arm.

A few seconds later, Leo Saint-Clair shuddered, sighed, and opened his eyes. The right one was slightly masked by the slanting bandage. His three comrades, the two other men and the young woman saw his face express astonishment at first, then amazement, and then a frightful terror, while his clear brown eyes rolled madly in their orbits.

Robert Champeau, more impulsive than his companions, could not help taking a forward step toward the bed and exclaiming: "What is it, Leo? What's wrong?"

With a vigorous thrust of his supple hips, Saint-Clair sat up; his half-extended arms moved, his hands seemingly groping for invisible objects. With a brutal emotion, they all heard him say, in a tremulous voice: "Everything's dark! Black! I can no longer see! I'm…oh, my God! I'm blind!"

"No, my friend, no, you're not!" said the doctor to Champeau, taking him by the arm and forcing him backwards—and he seized the wounded man's groping hands himself, pronouncing in a firm and benevolent voice: "Monsieur Saint-Clair, listen to me! Be calm and strong, and listen to me! No, you're not blind, and you won't be. The person who's talking to you is Doctor de

Villiers-Pagan. You're in a room in my clinic in Lausanne. Your comrades are here, safe and sound. You have a wound on the right side of your head, along the temple, level with the eye—an insignificant wound that will scar over within three days—but the impact of the bullet that struck you occasioned such a brutal shock to your ocular nerves that it has caused a temporary overload. That's all…nothing more. Do you believe me? You must believe me, because it's the exact truth."

With that immense and profound statement, he fell silent.

While the surgeon had been talking, though, Saint-Clair's face had cleared and become calm; his eyes became still. His entire physiognomy no longer expressed anything but a keen attention, an intelligent desire to understand and to believe. Finally, a smile even spread over his lips, which had become firm and ruddy again, and it was in his normal voice—steady, decisive and still quite incisive—that the young man said, slowly: "Thank you, Monsieur. I believe you. But how are my friends? Robert and René have been attacked, struck down. And there's nothing wrong with Jean?"

Monsieur de Villiers-Pagan stood aside then, and made a gesture that the three young men understood. They hastened to the bedside of their Chief and friend, and for a few minutes, while their hands enlaced and their breath overlapped, there was a noisy mixture of ardently amicable, confident, encouraging words, concluded by an affirmation from Saint-Clair: "We've lost the first round. We'll win the second, and also the last! May I recover my sight swiftly! As for the rest of my being, body and soul, I feel more vigorous and lucid than ever!"

He laughed, and his comrades laughed too, with happiness and hope. In the silence that followed, however, as is usual after an explosion of strong emotion, the voice of Doctor de Villiers-Pagan rose up, reticent and slightly hesitant, like that of a man expressing an idea that has just occurred to him, and with which he has astonished himself.

"Will you please stand still where you are, Monsieur Le Breuil, and you, gentlemen. I won't budge either. Would you, Aurora, close the window completely, both the internal and external shutters, and pull the curtains, hooking them together. There needs to be total darkness in here..."

Everyone was surprised.

"Is it an experiment?" murmured General Le Breuil. His voice was cautious and low, but everyone heard him, including Saint-Clair.

"Yes," the surgeon replied. "There's something astonishing and exciting in the iris and the pupil of those eyes. They weren't like that before the trauma—they couldn't have been. They're dilated; they have a sort of internal coloration, if I might put it that way, which makes the normal shade more transparent. They remind me of the eyes of a lynx at dusk, or he eyes of certain nocturnal birds. Hurry up, please, Aurora!"

The young woman had only two more actions to perform to make the room dark—completely, opaquely dark—for double shutters and thick curtains had been provided for certain circumstances in which invalids needed to be in total darkness even during the hours of daylight.

There was an exclamation then—a sharp and resonant exclamation, uttered by Leo Saint-Clair. The exclamation was followed by words proffered in a tone that became increasingly exultant and excited.

"I can see! I can see clearly! In this darkness, oh my God! I can see! You there, Mademoiselle, very pale. And you, Champeau, you Croqui, you Degains! And you, Monsieur, presumably Doctor de Villiers-Pagan, as you introduced yourself a few minutes ago. And that other gentleman over there, at the back of the room. I can see, I can see clearly! And it's really dark? Absolutely dark? Yes, undoubtedly, since you ordered it thus. Ah, I'm a nyctalope, a nyctalope! Is it possible? Yes, it must be, since I'm experiencing it and know perfectly well that I'm not delirious, that I'm not mad, and I'm in full possession of my reason and lucid control of my senses!"

The impassioned voice fell silent.

In the darkness, in which no one but Saint-Clair could see anything, there was nothing for an entire minute than the painting breath of the prodigious nyctalope, overwhelmed by emotion. Then his voice resounded again, hesitant and fearful now. "But tell me, Doctor, tell me...what you initially affirmed, which is that I'll be able to see as usual—which is to say, in broad daylight—that will be realized too, won't it? And I'll still be able to see in the dark? Come on, Doctor, please tell me what you think. You can't see me, but I can read in your face the exaltation of a great discovery. What do you think? Speak, speak, I beg you..."

He fell silent, breathing even harder than before.

And he and saw and heard—and everyone else in the room heard—Doctor Adrien de Villiers-Pagan, whose encyclopedic medical and surgical knowledge was famous throughout the world, affirm with certainty: "The chiasma of the optical nerves is among the most astonishing marvels that the life of the human body offers us. That chiasma, that swelling of the optical threads that make up the vital system, the generator, the accumulator, the condenser and the distributor of visual power, is still a mystery in several of its actions and reactions. I can't, therefore, explain *a priori* the phenomenon of which you are, so far as I know, the first human example. As for explaining it *a posteriori*, I could only do that by dissecting you alive...and even then...at the first contact with my scalpel, the marvel would be annihilated, and I'd only find myself confronted by a chiasma like those I've seen many times before in the course of my anatomical studies. No, I can't explain anything!" He took a deep breath, then resumed, with the same forced calm: "But I can establish one fact, one precise, localized, demonstrative and evident fact. The darkness in this room is absolute, but you can clearly see the walls the furniture, the objects and the people who are here. Can you see us in full color? Answer me."

"Yes, in full color," Saint-Clair replied. "A trifle blurred, though, it seems to me."

"There it is! You can see in the dark. It's a confirmed fact. The shock produced on the chiasma of the optic nerves by the impact of the bullet sliding along the temporal bone has modified its equilibrium, perhaps even transformed the normal economy and he general faculties. You're a nyctalope, and that's a fact. Will it last? Will it be maintained when your natural diurnal clear-sightedness returns? That will come back, sooner or later. I won't hesitate to be frank with you, Monsieur, since you're evidently courageous. That, I simply don't know." He took another deep breath, and continued: "Yes, I don't know. We're witnessing a series of phenomena of which you are the living and conscious subject. How will that series evolve? I have no idea. Let's wait and see!"

And they waited—which is to say that, after a whole hour spent in recording, on Doctor de Villiers-Pagan's instructions, all the external manifestations of his nyctalopia, Leo Saint-Clair was bathed once again in the broad light of day, Mademoiselle Malianova having slowly and progressively unmasked, disengaged and opened the window.

"I can't see—I'm blind!" said Saint-Clair, with the stoical firmness of a man who has agreed with a stout heart to carry out redoubtable experiments, and to have them carried out upon him.

"Let's wait and see!" the scientist said, again.

They waited four days and five nights. Working in shifts, Monsieur de Villiers-Pagan, Robert Champeau, René Croqui, Jean Degains and even General Le Breuil kept watch on the wounded man, the invalid.

Lying down by night, standing up or sitting down by day, the latter slept, ate, read, performed Swedish gymnastic exercises and walked in his room or in the doctor's private garden, access to which was prohibited to the staff and patients of the clinic. As for Mademoiselle Aurora Malianova, she no longer came into the room, but she was the one who kept the blind Saint-Clair company in the garden while Croqui, Degains and Champeau were at the dining-table.

Leo Saint-Clair continued to see clearly in the dark, but was blind during the day. On the morning of the fifth day, however, at 11 a.m.—shortly after Champeau, Croqui and Degains had set off to eat breakfast, as usual, at the Hôtel du Pélican, where they had kept their rooms and where they hoped in spite of everything for the return or news of Wenceslas Polki—Mademoiselle Malianova heard a hesitant voice close at hand saying: "My God! Am I really awake? Isn't it a dream? The sky, those trees, those flowers, and that beautiful angelic face! Oh, is it possible?"

Feminine ears undoubtedly have special properties, for it was the words "that beautiful angelic face" that Mademoiselle Aurora heard, and it was a face rosy with apparent confusion that she lifted up—because she was reading at the time, with her head lowered. The confusion was immediately drowned by the enormous and rapid flux of a violent emption, a joy that made her laugh and cry out...perhaps to cry and laugh too loudly for it to be entirely sincere.

Standing before her, although he had been lying in a canvas deck-chair a few moments earlier with his eyes closed, Leo Saint-Clair was looking at her, with his eyes wide open, alive and joyful. And he was conscious of an almost painful, and yet exceedingly sweet, emotion that he had never experienced before. He blushed violently— but at that same moment, the young man found the measure of the self-mastery, self-possession and calmness of which he was capable.

He plunged a sharp, almost black gaze into the young woman's blue eyes, and he said, very softly: "Mademoiselle Aurora Malianova, isn't it?"

As if fearfully tremulous with surprise and joy, she seemed incapable of doing anything but stammer: "You can see, Monsieur...can you see?"

"I can see! And the first living being that I've seen again in broad daylight is you, Mademoiselle. In the dark, when I was the Nyctalope, you never came. I scarcely caught a glimpse of you during the first experiment...and now you, the first... Oh, I shall never forget it!"

He took her gently by the hand. As if subjugated, she abandoned herself to him. In order to kiss her, he lowered his head, and did not see the young woman's eyes become as hard and cold as a blade of blue steel, with an expression of hateful cruelty. When he raised his head again and looked at Mademoiselle Malianova, she smiled, pretending to be confused.

He smiled too, and said: "Would you care to take me to Monsieur de Villiers-Pagan, Mademoiselle? He ought to be the second one to know. And then, I'd like to find out for myself whether, while no longer being blind by day, I can still see clearly in the dark. I've got nothing against nicknames, when they're rich in meaning, and believe me, Leo Saint-Clair the Nyctalope will suit me very well!"

"Come on, Monsieur, quickly," she said, her voice warmly resonant.

A quarter of an hour later, in a tightly-sealed room, Leo Saint-Clair established that he was indeed, still and supremely, the Nyctalope.

"Oh, dear God, may I be so forever!" he exclaimed, raising his arms in a surge of enthusiasm and desire that animated his entire being. Immediately mastering himself, however, and turning to Champeau, Croqui and Degains, who had hastened in response to a brief telephone call from Mademoiselle Malianova, he said incisively: "Back to the hunt tomorrow, my friends! In the work we've undertaken, and which we've had to abandon for six days, it's a good omen nevertheless that our first defeat had had the consequence, for me of nullifying the ambushes, difficulties and impossibilities of darkness. To no longer have to take account of darkness, when we're fighting against men for whom material and moral darkness is a safeguard, is both an incessant superiority and a very encouraging symbol... From tomorrow on, we'll get back on the trail. If there's still time, it's necessary to save Polki, find Sadi Khan, and recover the plans and models of Radiant Z...and quickly!"

"Long live the Nyctalope!" cried Champeau.

Mad with enthusiasm and joy, the three "forwards" embraced their Chief without being able to see him. Doctor de Villiers-Pagan and General Le Breuil, who were very emotional, were smiling in the darkness—but the seemingly-discreet Aurora had left the room, perhaps having others things to do, carefully closing the door behind her on the darkness in which the two large clairvoyant eyes were gleaming.

Alive to the light and nyctalopian as those eyes were, however, they would never have been penetrating enough or powerful enough to see into the obscure soul of that enigmatic young woman, in whose presence Leo Saint-Clair had suddenly experienced the revelation of first love, and first desire...

# Part Two: Turnabout

## Chapter I: The Real Aurora

It is no secret for anyone in the world that some years before 1914, the German General Staff, in making preparations for an eventual war—as every good General Staff has to do—had organized a very well-constructed network of spies in France, Russia, England, Italy, the Balkans and Turkey, and that one of the nerve-centers of this network was a beautiful modern villa situated in Berne in Switzerland, on the road to Thoune, in the vicinity of the Nouveau Jardin Botanique. Nor is it a secret, either, that the various Russian terrorist, nihilist and anarchist organizations had their headquarters in Geneva, where the leaders of nihilism, terrorism, anarchy and Bolshevik communism, such as Lenin and Trotsky, were in virtually permanent residence—save for occasional sojourns in Paris and mysterious trips from which they did not always return—perpetually surrounded by more or less numerous "comrades" of both sexes.

As often happens, the various elements of these two organizations, so fundamentally different and sometimes so diametrically opposed, occasionally interpenetrated one another. And it was not uncommon for Russian terrorists, in order to fill their coffers and promote their own imminent or distant projects, to carry out espionage on behalf of Germany. On the other hand, it was just as frequent for German secret service and counter-espionage officers, in order to enrich the information of their General Staff, to pretend to be Polish anti-Tsarists or Jews animated by a spirit of vengeance against the Cossack executors of imperial pogroms, and to be engaged as informers or militants in revolutionary Russian organizations.

There were, in consequence, hybrid gangs composed of fake pro-German spies and fake Russian terrorists—or, rather, people who were simultaneously, or who alternated between, one thing and the other, and who served the High Command in Berlin or were obedient to Lenin and Trotsky according to their personal interests or their convictions—patriotic for some, revolutionary for others.

Lenin and Trotsky were unaware of these often-tragic imbroglios, but the German High Command was unaware of nothing, and had in its pay the secret chief of these gangs, the man whom all the police forces of Europe only knew by the presumably-false name of Theodore Wallis, supposed resident of Chicago, and by another name that could only be an enigmatic and suggestive soubriquet: Sadi Khan. It was also known, however, that the individual was marked on the forehead by a horizontal scar.

At any rate, while it can be affirmed that "Theodore Wallis" and "Sadi Khan" were names known to the police, no policeman had ever seen more than a name inscribed in a hotel register, the lease of a furnished house or some passport. The individual who used them, or to whom they were, at least attributed, always seemed to have vanished into thin air. There was no further evidence of his real existence except for one fact, evidently charged with enormous and incalculable consequences: Monsieur Pierre Saint-Clair had clearly seen the horizontal scar on the forehead of the fake Polish scientist who had wounded and robbed him, and destroyed his workshops, store-rooms and the results of twenty years' work, by means of time-bombs.

From then on, Theodore Wallis, or Sadi Khan, was a newly-marked man—but as, according to certain checks made by the second bureau of the French Ministry of War, that terrible and mysterious individual might very well have been both a former agent of the French counter-espionage service, who had disappeared after the still-inexplicable theft of Anglo-French diplomatic documents of the greatest importance, the greatest prudence had been prescribed in high places. And that was why the spontaneous entrance on to the field of battle by Leo Saint-Clair and his three friends had been so warmly welcomed; against Sadi Khan, the young men constituted an active element that, whatever happened, could be officially denied and disowned—denial and disavowal being a standard means, in certain delicate circumstances, of avoiding revelations and international humiliations that might be extremely dangerous to the maintenance of peace in Europe.

The consequence of this was that if Leo Saint-Clair and his companions did not succeed in thwarting Sadi Khan, or lost their lives in succeeding—which was, after all, a possibility—the French government would sacrifice them in the superior interest of the country. The four youths would be aided officiously, with the utmost discretion, but from the official and public point of view, they were unknown.

Such, in its various dimensions, was the "state of play" shortly after noon on the eleventh of March 1912, when Mademoiselle Aurora Malianova, quietly left the room in which Leo Saint-Clair had just established that, having ceased to be blind in daylight, he nevertheless remained clear-sighted in the dark.

March 11 was a Monday.

Every week, from noon on Monday to noon on Tuesday, Mademoiselle Malianova, nurse-secretary at Doctor de Villiers-Pagan's clinic, had the benefit of a day's leave. She was entirely free, during 24 hours, to do whatever she wished, whether to take her meals and sleep at the clinic, or to desert the nurses' refectory and her private room and go wherever she pleased, without any check-ups. Such were the clinic's terms of service for each of the seven nurses, among whom Mademoiselle Malianova occupied, not the first place—which was reserved for Madame Bliss, the matron—but a privileged position, by virtue of the fact that she was both the secretary and the customary assistant of the director, Doctor de Villiers-Pagan.

As noon chimed on that day, Monday March 11, therefore, Mademoiselle Aurora Malianova telephoned the matron from her room. "I'm going out until tomorrow, Madame Bliss. The weather's good. I'll take the ferry, eat lunch aboard, and go to spend my day off with my sister in Geneva."

"Have a good time, child," the matron replied, in her warmly maternal voice. "So, will you be lunching with us at noon tomorrow?"

"Yes, Madame."

With that, Mademoiselle Malianova hung up, took off her white smock—beneath which she was dressed for the town—substituted a little fur hat for her white-and-blue head-dress with the red cross, put on gloves and draped a light mantle over her left arm, picked up her hand-bag, and left her room and the clinic.

The young woman could certainly have left without telephoning the matron. It was her day off, for the employment of which she did not have to account to anyone. Since she had started working at the clinic eight months earlier, however, she had been careful not to hide any aspect of her life, which appeared to unsuspicious eyes to be as transparent as fine crystal.

Indeed, Mademoiselle Malianova did go to catch the ferry-boat from Vevey to Geneva, which called at Lausanne at twelve-thirty. There was a little restaurant on board—for "refreshments," as the Swiss said in those days. When the weather as mild, people could be served on little tables on the deck or the afterdeck, sheltered from the sun, if necessary, by an expandable awning— and it was always delightful to eat in the open air, to the dull rhythm of the boat's engine as it moved over the tranquil water.

And that day, Mademoiselle Malianova lunched with the heartiest and most discriminating appetite in the world. She was quite content, quite happy; and her beauty—ordinarily a trifle cold, as in so many Nordic beauties whose vivacity and profundity of intelligence match the perfection of their features—was revived and softened. Her blue eyes seemed more mischievous than hard. A disinterested observer might have thought that the young woman, while eating and drinking, was indulging in a meditation not exempt from satisfied vanity, spiced with irony.

The boat's disembarkation-point was in Geneva harbor, opposite the Jardin du Lac.

Walking with a long and lithe stride, Aurora Malianova went diagonally through the garden to arrive at the exit to the Rue Pierre-Fatio, on the Grand-Quai du Lac, Then, following that street along the shore, she reached the Rive neighborhood, which forms an irregular trapezium in which many small and winding streets intersect in a sort of labyrinth. Without hesitation, although she turned round abruptly several times, as if to make sure that she was not being followed, the young woman went into the labyrinth and moved through it; it must have been quite familiar to her.

Suddenly, she disappeared—which is to say that anyone following her would have lost sight of her in the blink of an eye.

As she strode rapidly along the narrow sidewalk of a little deserted street, she had made an abrupt left turn, hurling herself into a low, dark porch, at the back of which, with as much skill as speed, she opened a door by means of a key that had been glistening in the fingers of her right hand for about a minute.

Having crossed the threshold and carefully relocked the door, Mademoiselle Malianova found herself in darkness, but she reached out with an accustomed gesture and pressed a button with her index finger. An electric light came on, at the end of a thread hanging down from an upward-sloping ceiling, beneath which extended the narrow steps of an old stone staircase, at the far end of a narrow corridor.

The young woman went up those stairs.

On the landing—the house only seemed to have one story at that point—Mademoiselle Malianova knocked on a door: two quick raps, three slower ones, one last louder rap, and finally a scratch.

There was a brief delay, and then the door opened, revealing a man, who immediately said, in a serious voice, speaking Russian: "Good day, my beloved Katyushka."

"Good day, darling!" Throwing her arms around the man's neck, the young woman planted a long kiss on his lips, and then stepped away, laughed, and took two or three steps forward.

She found herself in a vast low-ceilinged room, relatively poorly lit by a single window overlooking the low roofs of little houses and shops, but comfortable, pleasant and very intimate, doubtless by virtue of the profusion and richness of the Oriental carpet that covered the entire floor and the walls, draping a large and low divan-bed strewn with multicolored cushions. The furniture comprised a large table in the middle, laden with papers, files and books, a cupboard with sculpted wood panels, bookshelves loaded with volumes, two large leather-upholstered armchairs and four poufs similarly clad in leather. In spite of the fresh air entering through the open window, the atmosphere was impregnated with the odors of Oriental tobacco and Armenian paper. Indeed, there was a lidless lacquered box on the corner of the table, filled with cigarettes, along with a copper bowl half-full of cigarette-ends and a Chinese incense-burner  from which thin wisps of blue smoke were escaping.

After carefully closing and bolting the door, the man pulled a heavy Karamanian door-curtain across it and rejoined Aurora, whom he had addressed as Katyushka—an affectionate diminutive of the Russian forename Katia. He was a tall, broad-shouldered fellow with a Kalmuk-like head, with prominent cheekbones, thin, clearly-defined lips, close-shaven to expose slightly hollow cheeks and a square chin. His eyes, of an indefinable color, deeply buried beneath thick eyebrows, shone with a yellow gleam. Delighted by the anticipated visit, he laughed, and his magnificent white teeth sparkled in his swarthy face. He might have been 40 years old. He was dressed in grey-flannel tennis trousers and a shirt made of the same cloth, open at the neck. A narrow leather belt was tightened about his supple waist, neatly proportionate to his height and the broadness of his shoulders. In brief, he was a splendid athlete, but his physiognomy must sometimes have been disquieting.

For the moment, that physiognomy only expressed happiness, while he grabbed the young woman's head gently in both hands, towering over her and leaning down so that he could kiss her on the lips again.

With a rebellious laugh, though, Katia escaped and pirouetted toward the window. She threw her hat and gloves on the divan, where she had already set down her handbag and mantle. Then, suddenly becoming serious, she closed the window.

The man's face hardened, and his voice was hushed as it asked: "Why?"

She came back to him. Standing between the table and the divan, they were facing one another. She raised her head slightly, while he lowered his own, and their gazes met, equally serious.

"I have important things to tell you, Grigoryi. But first, do you know what happened a week ago?"

"With regard to…?"

"With regard to Sadi Khan and Radiant Z?"

"And how do you know that something happened?" asked Grigoryi, not suspicious but very interested.

"Answer me first, my darling," she said, with gentle authority. "It will be clearer, and we won't have to repeat things."

"All right!" And without hesitation—which proved that the mature man had absolute confidence in the young woman—Grigoryi spoke, still in a hushed and calm tone. "Sadi Khan seriously wounded the engineer Saint-Clair; then he took possession of the plans, notes and scale models of Radiant Z. Afterwards, he destroyed the inventor's laboratory with a bomb. He was able to get away. On the night of the fifth and sixth he came here. He gave me the plans, the notes and the models and ordered me to get to work on the theory, the manipulation and the probable effects. I haven't had any news of him since." He fell silent.

"That's all?" said Katia.

"Yes."

She shivered with excitement, put her two long and beautiful hands on the man's shoulders and said, in a contained but ardent voice: "Well, pay attention! We've got a fight on our hands."

"Oh! What is it that you know? It's your turn—speak!"

"Naturally, my darling, Well, the inventor's son, Leo Saint-Clair, has set off on a campaign to avenge his father and recover the documents and the models. Three of his friends are with him. A Polish agent from the second bureau of the French Ministry of War was attached to them—a man named Wenceslas Polki, known as Wen.

"Last Wednesday, this Wen must have taken advantage of certain things he knew or suspected, and must have gone straight to the Maison-Blanche after leaving the Hôtel du Pélican, where Leo Saint-Clair had taken up residence on his arrival, the night before. I don't know how, but Wen was captured there, where he expected to be the captor. As chance would have it, just as the Pole called for help inside the Maison-Blanche, Leo Saint-Clair and his companions were passing by on the road, in a car. They recognized the desperate voice. They went into the house, Brownings in hand. There was a fight—but the victory was ours. They all got away, some by boat, others in Saint-Clair's own car, taking Wen with them!"

"Bravo!" Grigoryi put in. His face had become increasingly animated since the young woman had begun her story.

"Wait!" she said. "There's more!"

"Oh!"

"Yes. As they fled, one of ours, in the car…"

Without omitting a single relevant detail, but also without wasting a single word, Katia recounted the consequences and the conclusion of the dramatic adventure.

At the end—the very end—the tall, strong and mature Grigoryi burst out laughing, slapping his sides. "Ha ha! A nyctalope! Like a cat, like an owl, like a lynx! But that's magnificent! The boy must be very proud. Let's hope, furthermore, that he's fallen in love with his blonde, blue-eyed nurse, eh? For he must be all of 20 years old, this paladin!"

Leaning both hands and her back on the edge of the table, however, Katia remained serious. She let the mocking hilarity, vibrant with challenge, die down of its own accord. Then, simply, but in a tone and with a gaze that imposed themselves on the man, she said: "My dear Grigoryi Alexandrovich, you're wrong to laugh. Leo Saint-Clair is, indeed, 20 years of age, and his companions are about the same age, but he's no child, nor are the others. I've spent four long days beside him. I've got him to talk. Grigoryi, my love, my master, believe me when I tell you that Leo Saint-Clair bears within him the signs of a great destiny. He will be—he already is—an exceptional man. You know that I can often read men's souls, and that the unknown God has endowed me with an intuitive sense that is sometimes completed by the faculty of second sight..."

She interrupted herself, and the color of her blue eyes deepened to become a somber and profound, strangely velvety azure. Facing her, the man seemed to have subsided. Then his coarse face took on a singularly timid expression, as if his subjugated mind had entered a limbo of unconscious veneration and irresistible fear.

After a silence that seemed to weigh down upon the man and oppress him further, Katia continued peremptorily: "Well, Grigoryi, I'm convinced that without me, neither you nor Sadi Khan, nor your entire gang combined, will triumph over Leo Saint-Clair, who is as entitled to be called the Nyctalope by symbolism as by reality."

She turned slightly to one side, showing off her bust, molded by her figure-hugging jacket, took a cigarette from the box and struck a match.

Grigoryi gradually straightened up again. His face resumed the rudely serious expression that must have been habitual to it. He put his hands in his pockets, took a step forward, and said, simply: "What should we do now, Katyushka, in your opinion?"

"I don't know," she replied, having launched a cloud of grey smoke toward the ceiling. "No, I don't know yet. But what about you, darling? What have you got out of your examination of Radiant Z?"

He frowned and said, bitterly: "Nothing!"

"Really?" she said, in surprise.

"Nothing, my darling. The engineer Pierre Saint-Clair is a prudent man. The plans stolen by Sadi are only fragmentary; the specifications lack three or four formulas that must be essential, and both the scale models of the apparatus include the same gap: the detector component isn't there. How and of what is it made? For it isn't an ordinary detector. I've already fabricated several in the dimensions required by the dimensions of the apparatus. I've also tried Branly radio-conductors[6] modified for the special properties of Radiant Z. I got no result. After five days of solid work, I'm exactly where I started: the engineer Saint-Clair's invention has not given up its secret. I can only hope..."

He fell silent, struck by the young woman's tender and ironic smile and the new gleam in her eyes. "What are you thinking, Katyushka?" he asked, timidly.

She laughed then, through her half-consumed cigarette into the copper bowl, and said in a clear and cheerful voice: "I'm certain, Grigoryi—certain, you hear—that Leo Saint-Clair knows all the secrets of Radiant Z. It's quite simple, therefore: either I'll get everything that the Nyctalope knows out of him myself, or, if I don't succeed, I'll bring the Nyctalope here, alone, and it will be up to you to get out of him what I wasn't able to obtain."

"Katyushka!" exclaimed Grigoryi, opening his arms.

"My darling...." And the young woman threw herself upon the man's breast with a voluptuous laugh.

---

[6] The radio-wave detector invented by Edouard Branly (1844-1940) in 1890 is better known as a coherer, although Branly called it a radio-conductor. It was an integral part of the apparatus used by Marconi and other pioneers and was still in use long after 1912.

## Chapter II: The Parameters of the Problem

In 1912, one could enter and leave Switzerland with no other formalities than those of putting one's baggage through customs. One did not have to make any declaration of identity, directly or indirectly, to the police. Foreigners were free to enter the country, to stay there on holiday or to take up residence, without having any other obligation than not contravening the laws applicable to Swiss citizens. That, together with its central position within Europe, the climatic and tourist attractions of the beautiful and picturesque country's various regions, and the limited resources that were necessary to live there without too many privations, was the reason why Switzerland was the more-or-less permanent refuge of a multitude of foreigners, many of whom were outlaws in their own country.

How was it possible, in the great universal caravanserai grouped around the lakes of Geneva, Neuchâtel, Zurich and the Four Cantons, to find men like Sadi Khan and his gang, who changed their names and physiognomies as easily as their clothes?

In the late afternoon of that Monday March 11, in the clinic's private drawing-room, in the presence of Doctor de Villiers-Pagan and General Le Breuil, who were very interested and excited by the extraordinary adventure to which Providence had made them witnesses of a sort, a veritable Council of War was held by Leo Saint-Clair, René Croqui, Robert Champeau and Jean Degains. The following day, the four "forwards" would be back in the field, the Nyctalope's wound having almost scarred over, no longer requiring anything more than a light bandage. Croqui's and Champeau's bruises were already forgotten.

By what means could they pick up a trail that they had lost completely?

It is necessary to mention that General Le Breuil, who was highly esteemed by the authorities in Lausanne and Geneva, had had a conversation with the police chiefs of the two cities. The latter were quite ready to consider the dramatic fight in the lakeside house as a criminal incident, and had hastened, when informed of it, to conduct immediate enquiries throughout their respective jurisdictions. The results of the inquiry were as follows.

Leo Saint-Clair's grey roadster had been found abandoned on the lakeside road near Nyon; the body-work was intact but all the more-or-less movable parts, principal or accessory, assembled around the engine-housing had been deformed, broken or even pulverized with hammer blows. Immediately alerted, Champeau had had the automobile sent to the best garage-mechanic in Geneva, who sent a foreman to the factory in Sochaux to bring back all the relevant spare parts. It was certain that the roadster, scrupulously repaired, would be at its owner's disposition by midday on Tuesday March 12.

The lakeside house, known as the Villa Chimène, belonged to a Genevan insurance company and had been rented furnished three months before, for a year—paid in advance—by an old lady. That person had used a letting agency, and was said to be a Belgian national named Madame Berthe Romain. As she had paid a year's rent in advance, without bargaining, non further information had been sought and the keys to the Villa Chimène had been sent to her immediately.

The house was quite isolated, its nearest neighbor being a small family hotel 1500 meters away. No one could say anything about the old lady, whom no one except the manager of the agency had ever seen, and the searches mounted by the police in the Villa Chimène showed that, although unknown individuals had eaten and slept in the now-suspect house several times in the previous three months, they had only eaten tinned goods and slept on beds without sheets or blankets. They had found not the slightest object or the tiniest sheet of paper that might provide any sort of clue.

The result of all this, of which he had been informed by General Le Breuil and his three comrades, was that Leo Saint-Clair, when he opened his Council of War, was able to set out the parameters of the difficult problem by saying: "Where and to whom has Sadi Khan taken to documents stolen from my father? We don't know. Under what names have Sadi Khan and his companions been living since entering Switzerland? We don't know. What has become of Madame Berthe Romain? The police have been unable to find out. Is Wenceslas Polki dead or alive? If the latter is the case, where is he being held? A mystery. What is the name of the motor-boat in which the criminals we surprised in the Villa Chimène fled, and where is it? An enigma. And that's all!"

Champeau added, with soft emphasis: "That *all* is composed of presently-insoluble questions—but since we're safe and sound at your side, and you've become more powerful, my dear Leo, we'll solve them."

"We must!" pronounced the Nyctalope, in his most incisive tone.

Leo Saint-Clair was animated by a new moral force, not only because of his prodigious nyctalopia but also by the fact that he had received a letter that his mother had written three days earlier in the afternoon post: a long letter giving rather good news of his father, whose life, at any rate, was definitely out of danger. Doctor Champeau could not yet guarantee the complete recovery of the engineer's scientific and creative faculties, but he was sure that there were very good reasons for hope in that regard.

"We must!" After pronouncing these words, which expressed all of his invincible will, Leo Saint-Clair looked at General Le Breuil. From that eminent man, who had been Professor of Strategy at the Ecole de Guerre in Paris, and who, having spent half the year since his retirement in Switzerland, knew the country very well, the sage and ardent young man expected fruitful ideas, advice and instructions.

Thus mutely interrogated, however, the General replied with evident sadness: "My young friend, I understand the meaning of your gaze. Alas, if I had had to summarize the problem, I would not have done so any differently from you—and there is nothing in that summary but unknowns. I don't know anything; I can't think of anything—and it's the same for my brother-in-law, with whom I spent a good part of last night discussing all this."

Doctor de Villiers-Pagan could only nod his head in acquiescence. Those words and that acquiescence were a confession of impotence.

"As for the Swiss police," the General went on, "they're continuing their search, but in my opinion, they've reached a dead end that has very high walls and no doors or windows. They won't find anything more."

"Well, General," said Saint-Clair, in a deliberate tone, I can see that my friends and I must count, first and foremost on the aid of Providence and our own resources. So be it! But we can at least ask you respectfully, with gratitude for all that you and the doctor have done for us, to give the young men that we are by comparison with both of you an assurance of aid, assistance, advice, friendship, and perhaps even refuge, if the necessity should arise."

General Le Breuil got to his feet and took Leo Saint-Clair's hands, very emotionally, and shook them affectionately.

"You and your comrades can count on us, my boy. Your appeal will never be made in vain."

Doctor de Villiers Pagan added:

"And if you're ever in the vicinity of Lausanne, and don't want to stay at a hotel, this house is yours, my friends. At my clinic, night and day, you'll find rooms ready, the table set and everything else you that might be useful to you on hand."

He too shook the hands of Leo Saint-Clair and his comrades.

"Thank you! Thank you!" said the Nyctalope. But when he and his three friends had overcome their emotion, he sat down, along with the General and his brother-in-law, and said: "Well, let's deliberate all the same. Let's revisit the questions I've posed one by one. In the light of the facts we have, we might see some hypotheses emerging, and one or more plans of action. Is that agreeable to you, General and Doctor?"

"Of course!"

"Yes, yes!"

"*All right!*" put in Degains.

And in an abruptly-calmed atmosphere, Leo Saint-Clair the Nyctalope, his three friends, the General and the doctor ardently set about reexamining all the parameters of the problem one by one, in order to extract their deepest essence. Naturally, it was Saint-Clair who took the lead.

## Chapter III: The Author of the Crime

On the evening of that same day, at precisely 10:47 p.m., in the middle of a performance at the Grand Theater in Geneva, a bomb was thrown from one of the boxes on the balcony into the midst of the orchestra stalls. By some extraordinary chance, it did not explode—but the burning fuse with which it was equipped continued to throw off showers of sparks while the bomb rolled along the central aisle. Cries of terror were released by the spectators who saw it, and panic began to break out.

Then a thunderous voice resounded: "Be quiet! Don't move! There's no more danger!" And in the central aisle, a tall man was seen to lift the round black bomb—whose fuse he had extinguished—above his head. Policemen and foremen came running. The man and the bomb disappeared within the variously-uniformed group that immediately formed around him, which headed rapidly for the nearest exit.

On the stage, meanwhile, the performance was interrupted, and actors and scene-shifters emerged from the wings to mingle with the individuals already on stage. All of them were perplexed and frightened. In the great silence that had fallen over the auditorium, from one end to the other, sounds of running and shouting were heard coming from the balcony corridor. This significant noise was brief, though; the unknown individual who had thrown the bomb must have reached one of the large staircases, and the pursuit continued beyond the acoustic range of the hall.

Then, from among the spectators occupying the orchestra stalls—almost all of whom were standing up—a calm and authoritative voice said: "Ladies and gentlemen, for the sake of the good name of the city of Geneva and its theater, the performance must continue."

There was an astonished silence, which lasted for a few seconds—then, suddenly, people cried out from all sides:

"Yes! Yes!"

"The gentleman is right!"

"Exactly! Bravo!"

Rising above the hubbub, the same calm and authoritative voice went on: "Messieurs the actors and Mesdames the actresses, we beg you to continue!"

There were more "Bravos!" and cries of "Yes! Yes!" There was also some nervous laughter, but it was all drowned out by a deluge of applause. Then there were cries of "Sit down! Sit down!" from all sides.

On the stage, the actors, actresses, stage-hands and mechanics retreated into the wings; only two remained, resuming their positions and their roles. A vibrant voice spoke out in an ironic tone, saying: "My compliments to you, who are so happy! As for me, my fate is decided in advance; since I have escaped madness, I have dedicated all the deliria of passion to you. You can, without conceit, be assured of my warmest gratitude!" For they were playing François de Curel's *La Nouvelle Idole*,[7] and had

---

[7] *La Nouvelle Idole* by François, Vicomte de Curel (1854-1928) was first produced in Paris in 1899, but might well have been playing in Geneva in 1912. The eponymous idol is science, of whose worship Curel did not approve at all. There does not appear to be any reason within the story for La Hire

reached the third scene of the second act, in which Louise Donnat and Maurice Cormier are alone before the public.

Offstage, however, beyond the auditorium, its accessory passages and its exits—in fact, outside the theater—a man was still running away. He was fleeing energetically, skillfully, rapidly and athletically, with prodigious self-composure. With his elbows and fists he had thrust aside the people in the corridors who had immediately set out in pursuit of him, who were soon joined by firemen, theater employees, and policemen in uniform and plain clothes, and also by various individuals who had emerged from the auditorium—several of whom, more alert or more calmly committed, had reached and joined the leading group. Meanwhile, the fugitive leapt up and down staircases, went around a security guard, planted a fist in the face of an usher, knocked over the ticket-collectors and got out of the theater.

To the south-west of the Place Neuve, the Promenade des Bastions extends between the Jardin Botanique and the gardens of the Académie. At that nocturnal hour, in the aftermath of winter, that district of Geneva was absolutely deserted. It was into the Promenade, and then into the meandering pathways of the gardens, that the fleeing man hurled himself. From the composite crowd that was following him, one faster individual became clearly detached, and that runner gained on the fugitive as he got further ahead of the howling crowd.

The runner eventually caught up with the fleeing man on a dark pathway, but he did not grab him or lay a

---

to cite it here, but he was not the sort of writer who valued aesthetic coherence—or, indeed, any other kind.

hand on him. "Don't be afraid," he said, quite clearly. "I'm a friend." And he began running alongside him. Then, breathlessly but precisely, he said: "I'm an even better runner than you. Follow me—I'll take the lead and I'll take you to a safe refuge. Do you hear me? Trust me. I approve of what you did, and I'm not the only one. Have confidence, comrade, and we'll save you. Tell me what country you come from, so that I can talk to you in your own language!"

"I entrust myself to you," panted the fugitive. "I'm French."

"Good! Know that I'm an amateur running champion, and I'll use all my resources!" The man made an effort, by virtue of which he pulled ahead. The chase increased his speed.

Behind them, already too far away, the crowd had lost its advantages. Howling curses and threats, it split up, dispersing along the railings of the Jardin Botanique and the breadth of the Promenade des Bastions, into the pathways and on to the lawns of the Académie gardens. Among the most advanced pursuers there was only one policeman; a forceful order, emitted by the familiar voice of a senior officer, had launched the rest of them into a transversal path bordering the American railway.

The result of this was that, when the fugitive and his guide emerged from the western side of the gardens into the Nouvelle Rue Saint-Léger, they could only hear the shouts of the pursuers as a distant rumor of scattered noises. The leader slowed down slightly, letting the other catch up with him, and said: "You're safe for now. At the end of the street, when we reach the Place des Philosophes, where there are always two policemen on sentry duty, we'll resume the normal pace of men who are quietly going home."

"Yes, yes!" panted the fugitive, who was showing the first signs of fatigue.

A quarter of an hour later, the two men went into a house that, at least for a time, might serve as their "home." That house was a villa in the Rue Sauter, in the south-western part of the new suburb of Saint-Palais. It was a well-to-do villa in the middle of a pretty little garden girdled by a high wall surmounted with railings, which was brightly illuminated by the moon, presently fully round and shining between two clouds.

They had gone into the garden by a service entrance that the runner had opened with a key extracted from one of his pockets. At the main door of the villa however, which was oddly masked by a tightly-knit clump three or four tall trees, the runner had to press his thumb on the button on an electric bell; he did not have a key to that door.

The two men waited on the doorstep in darkness— for a thick cloud had veiled the moon—for a full five minutes.

Finally, the door opened soundlessly and they went in. Immediately, the heavy batten closed behind them. They found themselves in a small, bare vestibule devoid of furniture, a carpet and wall-hangings, brightly illuminated by a ceiling-light, in which nothing could be seen at the far end but a door that was obviously made of thick, dense wood, so great was the impression of solidity it gave.

With the index finger of his right hand, the runner then rapidly made a sign in the air above his head, and pronounced, in a clear and emphatic voice: "1826!"

The door at the back immediately opened, and a man appeared on the threshold. He was short, thin and old, bare-headed and clean-shaven, dressed in a quilted dressing-gown and shod in red leather slippers. He had prominent blue eyes.

Then the runner said something at length in Russian.

The old man replied with a single word.

"Come on!" said the runner, immediately, taking the arm of the fugitive he had brought into this mysterious and rather astonishing refuge.

They crossed the threshold, from which the blue-eyed and clean-shaven old man stood aside in order to let them pass, and walked on. After taking several steps along a strangely semi-circular corridor, all three of them went into a large furnished room, which was comfortably—even luxuriously—fitted out as a study and library. The runner went first and the old man brought up the rear; as they entered, the runner and the fugitive removed their hats.

"Sit down," said the old man, in French. In the same language, he added: "Who is this young man, Vassily, and why have you...?"

"I don't know who the young man is Monsieur Roudine. I think he'll inform us himself, not of his identity, which is a matter of indifference to us, but as to his ideas and his objectives. What I do know is this, Monsieur Roudine: this young man has just thrown a bomb into the auditorium of the Grand Theater, in the middle of a performance."

"Oh!" said the old man, whose emaciated face brightened with pleasure, his large eyes glittering.

"Yes—and if it were not for the courage of one of those accursed police agents who are now creeping in everywhere, there would have been a fine marmalade of capitalists and bourgeois in Geneva tonight—but the agent grabbed the bomb and extinguished the fuse..."

"Young man," Monsieur Roudine put in, severely, "you have to throw a percussion bomb, which explodes on impact, or on turning upside-down. You're young. You lack experience. But that will come!"

"Outpacing the people who were pursuing the 'criminal'—who fortunately got out of the theater," Vassili went on, "I caught up with him and brought him...to shelter. He's a brother."

Then, for a long interval in which no one spoke, the young man was the object of Monsieur Roudine's and Vassily's inspection.

He was a tall, handsome fellow who could not have been more than 20 years of age—but he was only handsome by virtue of his stature and he harmonious proportions of his slim and muscular athletic body. His complexion was slightly jaundiced, as if he were unhealthy, and his face was covered with little red spots. His hair was thick, and so discolored that one could not tell whether it was black, brown or blond; it was like a dirty grey mane. There was no moustache of youthful down on his acne-marked upper lip, nor on his chin or his squamous cheeks. Furthermore, his eyes were hidden by round steel-framed spectacles with yellow-tinted lenses, solidly installed beneath arched eyebrows whose thin hair was indefinable in color.

The youth wore an extremely worn dark suit. His shoes were in good condition, but were of poor quality, with leather laces. The sleeves of his jacket, which were slightly short, revealed slim but solid wrists in perfect harmony with his long, sinewy hands, which were strongly-muscled. In sum, he was a young athlete, but his face was excessively unattractive unprepossessing and even slightly repugnant. The fellow could not be lacking in strength of mind, though, and was obviously self-confident, for, under the keen examination of Monsieur Roudine and Vassily—a typical "Russian student" nearing his 30th year—the enigmatic bomb-thrower maintained the straightforward and easy-going manner that he had assumed as soon as the breathlessness induced by his rapid and sustained flight had eased.

"Monsieur!" darted the old man—who, despite his evident collusion with "comrades," of whom Vassily was one, had evidently never adopted the intimate form of address habitual in anarchist and Russian nihilist milieux—"you must be French, since Vassily spoke to you in the French language in the vestibule. An affiliated anarchist?"

In a firm, incisive voice, the young man replied: "Anarchist, yes. Affiliated, no. Isolated, independent."

"Our comrade Vassily, Monsieur," Roudine went on, "has probably saved your life, and has, in any case, helped you very efficaciously. You don't owe him any gratitude, however, and you owe me no more for any aid that I might give you with respect to your ambitions and projects. Vassily was doing his duty to a comrade; I am doing and shall do mine. But you'll doubtless understand, of course, that before discovering your ambitions and your projects in order to help you to facilitate their realization, we need to be fully satisfied of being taken into your confidence—at least with regard to the plan of action that gave us the pleasure of seeing you here."

"That's perfectly natural," the young man replied, graciously enough, "but I'm not very eloquent. I don't know how to tell a story; I wander off the point and get lost. If you'd care to question me, Monsieur, I'll answer as best I can."

"Very good, very good!" said Monsieur Roudine, smiling broadly, while Comrade Vassily nodded his head approvingly—and, getting straight to the point that intrigued him most, the old man formulated his first question: "What led you to throw a bomb in the Geneva theater?"

The young man lowered his head. He waited a moment before replying. He was evidently concentrating his thoughts. Finally raising his forehead and looking straight through his tinted spectacle-lenses at Monsieur Roudine—slightly behind whom Comrade Vassily, seated on a high stool, opened his eyes excitedly—he replied in slow, curt and sometimes hesitant sentences.

"I won't hide anything from you, who have given me aid and assistance. My name is Adrien Fortis. My father was a cabinet-maker. After 30 years of hard work, he had amassed a little capital. He chanced to make the acquaintance of a wealthy wood-merchant, a speculator, who seduced him with promises of making a quick fortune. My father wanted to be rich in order to put me through the Ecole Polytechnique or Centrale, and then help me to acquire a strong position. He had invented a plating process that was as good as it was inexpensive. The speculator stole his savings and his profits, and, supported by a crooked contract, put him out of house and home, ruined. In despair, my father committed suicide. My mother died on the very same day, of a heart attack."

With these terrible words, Adrien Fortis yielded a strangle sob—but Monsieur Roudine asked abruptly: "What was the speculator's name?"

"His name was Maleste," the young man relied, hoarsely. "To avenge my father and mother, I killed him."

"Oh!" exclaimed Vassily, shivering with admiration.

"I've nothing to hide," Fortis repeated, having become calm again. "If you have the means you can make enquiries. Maleste's factories and villa are in Saint-Ouen, near Paris. The murder of the man passed for a base crime, for I emptied his pockets. That was justice. Then I left France, and under the assumed German name of Nierda Sitrof, a perfect anagram of Adrien Fortis, with false papers that I'd forged, I came to hide in Geneva. I continued my studies in private, but the sum I'd taken from Maleste's corpse wasn't very large. I ran out of money. I grew hungry. I lived for three months on things I found in trash-cans on the sidewalks, at dawn. I got some sort of blood-poisoning, which pitted my face with acne and infected my eyelids with a painful blepharitis. In the end, I decided to strike a great blow against bourgeois society and die..."

He sighed.

"Hence the bomb," said Monsieur Roudine, in a concentrated voice.

"Yes. With my last few *sous*, I bought shotgun powder. I spiced up it chemically with certain ingredients I was able to steal, by night, from a druggist's shop. From the deserted terrace of a café I also stole one of those hollow metal balls in which the waiters put their napkins and washcloths, and I made the bomb. I wanted it to claim as many victims as possible of the bourgeois class. That's why I threw it into the middle of the orchestra stalls at this evening's gala performance. The bomb was stuffed with fragments of cast-iron and lead, cut up with a saw. It would have been a fine massacre—but I hadn't anticipated that a man might have the courage to pick up the bomb and put out the fuse. He benefited from a prodigious stroke of luck, in any case, for the fuse was only set to burn for three seconds! That man put it out at the very end of the third second! Bah! That's fate…"

He fell silent. There was a long silence, during which Adrien Fortis, his head lowered again, rubbed his hands together nervously.

Suddenly, Monsieur Roudine said: "And I assume that you no longer want to die?"

Adrien Fortis raised his head, and pronounced, bitterly and terribly incisively: "Oh, no! No! Since I haven't succeeded in punishing bourgeois society for the harm that one of its own did to my father and myself, and for the harm it continues to do to people like me…" Carried away by a cold anger, he raised his clenched fists over his head.

What followed was simple and rapid.

Monsieur Roudine got up, took hold of the young man's fists and opened them, gently caressed the hands, which relaxed, and said, very softly: "My boy, for the moment you have more need of rest and sleep than anything else. I'll give you a mildly soporific potion to drink, which will set your nervous system to rights. Tomorrow, you'll appease your hunger for food and spend the day idling on the first floor of the house, where there's a library and where you'll have a bedroom. You'll have a bathroom at your disposal. Do you smoke? Yes? That's all right; I'll give you cigarettes, cigars and pipes. Rest, rest, rest—and recover all your mental and physical faculties. I'm a physician. I'll treat your blood infection and its dermal symptoms, and I'll cure your blepharitis. That's not all. In parallel, you'll be initiated into certain matters, introduced into a certain clan and adopted by it, and you'll be able to work on a plan for the destruction of bourgeois society—of which we, like you, are enemies—much faster and more efficacious that

that of individual and isolated direct action. Do you accept?"

"Oh, Monsieur!" cried Fortis, tremulous with joyful emotion.

"Good. Do you only speak the French language?"

"German too, quite well—my mother was from Alsace. I acquired the habit of talking to her in German from time to time. Poor woman! She had the ideas of an Alsatian woman with a French heart. She didn't believe in revenge. If not for Maleste, I would have become a man with my mother's ideas—but it's quite the contrary, at present."

"Very good, very good! Don't weaken, my friend. Souls like yours have Humanity for a fatherland! It's for the liberation of oppressed Humanity, for its revenge and for is happiness, that you must employ your exceptional faculties. Come on, shake hands with Comrade Vassily, who has saved you from filthy bourgeois 'justice' and come upstairs with me, where I'll set you up."

After Adrien Fortis and Vassily had exchanged a warm and cordial handclasp, Monsieur Roudine continued: "You're in no danger here. I'm Alexis Roudine, a knowledgeable and universally respected Egyptologist, very rich, very philanthropic and a trifle eccentric. That's my façade. What is behind that unassailable façade, which is virtually above suspicion, my lad, you'll soon find out, for you are worthy of it."

Twenty minutes later, lying in a good bed in a very pleasant room, having stretched out his arm to switch off the electric lamp beside the bed, the young Adrien Fortis sank into sleep, smiling—a smile so profound that his lips maintained its charming design all night long.

## Chapter IV: *"When You Mention the Wolf..."*

As usual on Tuesdays—this one was Tuesday March 12—Mademoiselle Aurora Malianova, having enjoyed her weekly day off, returned to the Villiers-Pagan Clinic in Lausanne shortly before noon.

She went straight to her room in order to relieve herself of her mantle, hat, gloves and handbag, and immediately telephoned the office of the Chief Medical Director, where a nurse fulfilling the role of temporary secretary and assistant was on duty.

"Hello? Mademoiselle Paschall?"

"Yes. I recognize your voice, Mademoiselle Malianova."

She laughed brightly. "Yes, it's me. Anything new?"

"No."

"The Boss is well?"

"Yes."

"Is he in a good mood?"

"Perfectly."

"Thanks! I'll have lunch, and I'll come and relieve you in an hour, my dear Paschall."

"Understood, beautiful Aurora."

Two bursts of young laughter fell into the telephone, and the receivers at either end were hung up.

Under the authority—rather indulgent and maternal outside business hours—of the windowed Madame Bliss, the clinic's matron, all but a few of the nurses who were on duty or off, according to the day, took their meals in a small and neat refectory which received daylight through a pair of large double-pained French windows overlooking the residents' garden. The female nursing staff of the Villiers-Pagan Clinic comprised a dozen full-time qualified nurses and six part-time trainees.

That Tuesday, the company at the midday meal numbered fourteen: nine qualified nurses, including Aurora, and five trainees. The meal was served at 12:15 p.m. and could be extended until 1 p.m. Then they had an hour's free time, to return to their own rooms, to congregate in the room set aside for reading and correspondence, or to walk in the garden.

When Mademoiselle Malianova went into the refectory, thirteen women were sitting around a long rectangular table, at one end of which the tall, wide and buxom Madame Bliss was enthroned.

"Ah, here's Aurora!... Aurora.... Mademoiselle... Good day... How are you?... Are you hungry?... Good weather we're having, yesterday and this morning... Have you been lucky enough to take advantage of it?... How is your sister?"

All of these remarks, and others, took flight while Mademoiselle Malianova made a circuit of the table, starting with Madame Bliss, shaking hands, smiling and speaking politely. Finally, she sat down, and they "attacked the starter."

Afterwards, during the brief lapse of time in which they waited for the two serving-women to serve the main course, each making a half-circuit of the table, they chatted, as usual. It was also usual for the nurse who was coming back from her day off to ask the ritual question, addressing herself primarily to Madame Bliss: "Is there anything new in the house?"

It was always the matron who answered first. Once the recent news had been imparted, until the end of the meal, everyone as at liberty to indulge in one-to-one or general conversation, with neither constraint nor formality, the general ambience, so far as the nurses in the refectory were concerned, traditionally being one of individual independence, reciprocal courtesy and universal good humor. So, also having personal reasons for not missing out on the habitual rite, Mademoiselle Malianova asked: "Is there anything new in the house?"

It was obvious that Madame Bliss was expecting the question. She replied immediately, with her customary complacency, but with an imperfect and fragmentary knowledge of events: "New? Yes, indeed. That handsome young Frenchman—his name's Leo Saint-Clair, isn't it?—is no longer in the clinic. He left yesterday afternoon, with his friends, at 6 p.m."

"Ah!" said Aurora. She needed all her self-composure not to betray her immense surprise, in which there as a good deal of disappointment. In the most natural tone that she could contrive, she said: "That's not surprising. The wound on his temple has almost healed, and there was nothing in his general state of health to prevent him leaving." While she served herself from the tray that the serving-woman offered to her, she added: "Nothing else?"

"No," replied Madame Bliss. "Nothing new in matters of duty. But yesterday evening at the theater—that bomb! We were only able to cast an eye over the newspapers. What are they saying about it in town?"

From then until the end of the meal, the conversation was desultory, sometimes individual and sometimes general, and concerned the outrage in the Grand Theater—about which Aurora, prudently reserved, claimed to know nothing, because she had not left her sister's side, had not gone into town and had not read the newspapers. After the dessert and the regulation cup of coffee, Mademoiselle Malianova retired to her room—but she was unable to settle down to anything there. Disconcerted and irritated, she stamped her feet and threw away the Russian cigarettes that she smoked nervously, without finishing them, until the impatiently-awaited time came for her to go back on duty. The bomb at the Grand Theater? A solitary anarchist, no doubt, since Grigoryi had not said anything about it.

The "departure" of Leo Saint-Clair upset the clever and diabolically perfidious plan that she had agreed with Grigoryi Alexandrovich to lead the son of the engineer Pierre Saint-Clair into a trap in the Rive neighborhood. She was therefore wounded in her feminine vanity—for she had clearly seen the violent and profound impression that her beauty had made on the young man—and, at the same time, furious at the unforeseeable difficulty and cruelly disappointed with respect to her hopes of rapid and complete success.

*I'd very much like to know why he left, and where he and his three companions have gone!* she said to herself.

Her mind was tense as she went to the directorial office. As she did every day, she had to wait there for Doctor de Villiers-Pagan at 2 p.m., after taking over from the temporary secretary. The latter was a cheerful and pretty 25-year-old native of Bern, romantically named Dorothy Paschall. She "handed over" to the full-time secretary, and rushed off to eat with the nurses in the "guard-room," for she was very hungry, despite the optional milk chocolate of which she had partaken, as a precaution, at 11 a.m.

Mademoiselle Malianova was not alone for long in front of the forms, files and round schedules in the directorial office. She had only been there five minutes when Monsieur de Villiers-Pagan came in. He was serious, absorbed and rather distant, as usual, but extremely soft-spoken and courteous, speaking in a steady, tranquil and benevolent manner.

"Good day, Monsieur Medical Director!" the nurse said, ritually, as she got up.

"Good day, Mademoiselle. A pleasant day off? Yes? Perfect." Immediately, in the most normal tone of professional communication, he continued: "Our interesting Nyctalope has departed. He's going back to France with his comrades. Our care would have been superfluous henceforth. A strange boy, who has become a phenomenon that I would have liked to study further, at leisure—but he's promised to come back in a few weeks. On his behalf, Mademoiselle, I renew the prescription of absolute secrecy regarding everything that concerns Monsieur Saint-Clair and the adventure in which circumstances have presently embroiled him. That's understood, isn't it?"

"Yes, Monsieur," stammered Aurora, slightly disconcerted by the evidence that a window of opportunity had closed in front of her and that it would be very difficult, if not impossible, to open it again.

Should she question Monsieur de Villiers-Pagan? No one ever did that. It would be so unusual that the anomaly might give rise to suspicions. She had, therefore, to keep quiet. Was the matter going to rest there? Yes, at least for the moment—for the medical director went on, as simply and peremptory as ever:

"Let's see. Bring the round schedule for Ward Three. We've done an appendectomy this morning; the patient has been pout in room eight. Come on!"

Mechanically obedient to the normal rules, the nurse opened a cupboard and took out a bonnet, a smock and a pair of rubber gloves, all of which were immaculate, having come directly from the autoclave and the linen-room. Monsieur de Villiers-Pagan did likewise, and the both went out of the directorial office to go, as they did every afternoon, to do their simple duty as physician and assistant nurse.

Now, this is why Leo Saint-Clair and his three companions had left the clinic in which he had become "the Nyctalope" at 6 p.m. the previous evening.

At the Council of War held between the four young men, General le Breuil and Doctor de Villiers-Pagan, Saint-Clair had said: "Let's deliberate. Let's take the questions one by one. In the light of the facts we have, we might see some hypotheses emerging, and one or more plans of action." Then, everyone had talked freely. Each intelligence made its contribution. The deliberation lasted three hours, and it was at the beginning of the third hour that the light finally dawned, astonishing, admirable and with divine clarity, in Leo Saint-Clair's mind.

The idea that had just occurred to him was a fecund amalgam of everything that had been said thus far; it was as ingenious and wise in reality as it was crazy and harebrained in appearance. It was audacious and original, and its execution involved terrible dangers. Gradually, however, experience, the official connections in Switzerland of the general, science and the exterior means of Monsieur de Villiers-Pagan contributed to the equipment of the idea of genius with a shape that rendered it, in the final analysis, acceptable and practicable. When all the numerous, complicated and delicate details of its execution were finally in place, the session was ended, after everyone had made a solemn oath only to reveal the resolutions that had been taken to those individuals who were directly involved in the plan's execution.

"I shall succeed," said Leo Saint-Clair, coldly, "unless death prevents me—that alone will be capable of it." Suddenly becoming cheerful, he added: "Bah! One doesn't die at 20!"

The Nyctalope spent an hour in Doctor de Villiers-Pagan's private laboratory. When he came out again, the upper part of his face was concealed beneath the pulled-down brim of a fur hat, and a muffler was pulled up almost as far as his eyes. In the meantime, General Le Breuil went to use the telephone in his brother-in-law's private apartment.

During that hour, Champeau, Croqui and Degains went to pick up the automobile, the grey roadster, which had been restored to good working order. They had paid the bill at the Hôtel du Pélican and recovered their luggage.

In the entrance-yard of the clinic, the four young Frenchmen had embarked in their vehicle, which drew away in the midst of cries of "Thanks!... *Au revoir!... A bientôt!...* Thanks!... Thanks!... We'll give your regards to Paris!... We'll be back!... *Au revoir!*"

Immediately after this departure, General Le Breuil and Monsieur de Villiers-Pagan had gone separately to Geneva, where each of them had important visits to make.

Meanwhile, the grey roadster did not go across the Swiss-French border, as everything had implied; it did not even go into Geneva. Nor far from the town, in the vicinity of the locale known as "Les Paquès," the automobile suddenly slowed down.

"Anything?" asked Saint-Clair.

"Nothing!" declared Degans, who was inspecting the section of road visible behind the vehicle.

Then Saint-Clair made a sharp right turn into a small by-road, passed under a narrow bridge over which the railway ran, accelerated, climbed a steep slope, turned left, and rapidly went into a paved courtyard surrounded by high walls and bordered at the back by a large, high and square building reminiscent of a barracks—but a barracks whose windows had all been fitted with orange canopies and decorated with flowers.

Behind the automobile, the double-battened gate of iron-reinforced wood was closed by a man in a green uniform trimmed with red.

The grey roadster rolled swiftly to the left of the house, and went around it to stop, beyond a lawn garnished with thick shrubbery, in front of a little chalet in the Swiss style. There, on descending from the car, Leo Saint-Clair was met be a white-haired gentleman with gold-rimmed spectacles, who shook his hand and said:

"Welcome, Monsieur. At the request of Monsieur de Villiers-Pagan and General Le Breuil, I'm putting this chalet at the disposal of the four of you. You'll find everything that the general listed on the telephone inside. There's a garage in rear deep enough and broad enough for your car. I'll leave you, gentlemen, for I have a lot to do. I'll come to see you again in an hour's time."

"Thank you, Monsieur!" said Saint-Clair.

The hospitable old man in the gold-rimmed spectacles and white hair was the famous professor of psychology Ambroise Dorsang, the proprietor and director of a private hospital known as the Sanatorium du Bouchet, where the mental illnesses of rich individuals of both sexes from all over the world were treated.

It was in one of the most comfortable chalets of the Sanatorium du Bouchet that Leo Saint-Clair took refuge at seven fifteen in the evening of Monday the eleventh of March—a refuge which, according to every appearance and by virtue of a sound logic, was doubtless intended to remain absolutely secret.

At the clinic in Lausanne, however, Mademoiselle Aurora Malianova—called Katia or, more intimately, Katyushka in other milieux—had not given up trying to discover the key to the enigmatic departure of Leo Saint-Clair and his companions. Being very intuitive, like so many Russian women when they are intelligent, amorous, passionate and fanatical, she did not believe that the four young men had returned to Paris.

Throughout the afternoon, as usual, she fulfilled her duties as a nurse-assistant and secretary to the Director to perfection, but her brain was nevertheless active, and she came to a decision.

When she finished work in the directorial office at 6 p.m., before bidding her usual "Good night" to Monsieur de Villiers-Pagan, she said, with considerable skillfully-feigned timidity and well-simulated anxiety: "Monsieur... Monsieur Medical Director..."

"What is it, Mademoiselle?" asked the doctor, slightly surprised but with his usual benevolence.

"My sister in Geneva isn't well. She's suffering a bout of cardiac trouble that's worrying me greatly. I'm not on duty tonight. I ask your permission to go watch over my sister until tomorrow morning."

Monsieur de Villiers-Pagan was a genuinely good man. He immediately became interested. "Has she a doctor?"

"Yes, a cousin by marriage, from the Russian colony. It's him, in fact, who prescribed that—at least for tonight, when the crisis will each its height—that someone attentive and experienced...he can't do it himself; he's not free. An unfamiliar nurse? Pooh! Especially when I..."

"Very well, Mademoiselle, very well!" There and then, the Medical Director filled in and signed a blank form giving permission for an overnight leave for Mademoiselle Malianova.

Less than two hours later, having taken the 6:30 train from Lausanne to Geneva, the young woman opened the door under the dark porch and went upstairs to knock on the door of the only apartment contained in the house hidden amid a crowd of disparate buildings in the Rive neighborhood.

As on the previous day, the tall broad-shouldered man came to open it.

"You, Katyushka!"

"Me, darling!"

She embraced him quickly, but only allowed herself to be half-embraced, so preoccupied was she. "Close the door again. Good! Come, listen to me!" And she recounted what she had learned regarding the departure of Leo Saint-Clair and his companions. That was little enough, in quantity, but how weightily it was charged with deception, perhaps with threat!

Grigoryi swore, thumped the table with both fists and said, rudely: "We need to know where they've gone and where he is—the inventor's son, assistant and collaborator. We need him. I've been working all day again, and I'm firmly convinced that we won't get anywhere, in spite of the plans, instructions and models. Something essential is missing, and I don't know what it is!" After a brief pause he added: "Do you, Katia, who have seen them, who have talked to Saint-Clair, and who know Villiers-Pagan well—the nuances of truth, lies or merely the restriction and dissimulation of his speech—believe that the four Frenchmen have crossed the border?"

"No!"

The young woman made that response without hesitation, in a tone of the firmest conviction.

"Then we must search for them without losing a minute," Grigoryi said. "Is it cold outside?"

"Yes."

"I'll take my cloak, then. Let's go out. We'll go to dinner, since there's nothing for the two of us to eat here, and then we'll go to Serge Ivanov's. There's a meeting tonight. We'll find comrades there who'll be able to start searching immediately. Four young Frenchmen equipped with an automobile like theirs have no chance of passing unnoticed—especially in Switzerland, where there are so few of them.[8]

The Caucasian Serge Ivanov, condemned to death three times over in his absence in St. Petersburg, was the secret leader of the active Central European organization of Russian nihilists known as the "flying squads." In Geneva, he was believed to be exercising the profession of medicine, in which he had a diploma from the University of Lyon. That explained the numerous visits he

---

[8] La Hire inserts a footnote here to remind his readers that the story is set in 1912, when automobiles were still relatively remarkable luxury items.

made in his neighborhood and the even more numerous ones he received. He was scrupulously submissive to all the laws and regulations that regulated the profession of physician by a foreigner in Switzerland. He paid his rent, his suppliers and his taxes very dutifully, and was never seen at any kind of political meeting. He was thus protected by the very laws of the country, and within the shelter of that safety he simultaneously carried out espionage of behalf of Germany and disseminated anarcho-terrorist propaganda against Russian Tsarism, world Capitalism and the Imperialism of bourgeois States.

He lived in an old house in the middle of the Rive quarter, between a courtyard and a garden, each of which was on a different street. It was a very comfortable dwelling in every respect. He lived alone, with an old German cook and a young Chinese valet. He was a man of middle age, quite ordinary in his general appearance, but with one particular distinction that was fairly rare in Europe and gave him an original physiognomy: he wore a beard in the old Yankee mode—which is to say, thickly covering the entire chin, while the lips and the upper parts of the cheeks were clean-shaven. It should be noted that such a beard can be removed within a minute with four strikes of a razor, and that the appearance of the face is then so radically modified as to be unrecognizable.

Every Tuesday, from nine p.m. until midnight, Doctor Serge Ivanov received his friends. In reality he held a council of espionage and anarchism. Admission to these Tuesday meetings was, in fact, restricted to comrades who combined the two functions of spy and revolutionary. The others, who did not know about the meetings, were only received or visited individually. Like a Talleyrand or a Lenin—to take examples from the opposite poles of political action—Serge Ivanov knew how to move men like pawns on a chessboard, without ever being captured himself, his own game only ending in a natural death after its conclusive success.

When the beautiful Katia and the colossal Grigoryi, having given the password, were admitted by the Chinese valet into the large drawing-room on the ground floor of Doctor Serge Ivanov's comfortable dwelling, the master of the house still had only three men and one old lady with him, for the hour was not advanced. Ordinarily, the meeting comprised 15 individuals, including Ivanov himself.

There was the usual exchange of cordialities between the "comrades" and, once the newcomers were sitting down and had each taken a cigarette from a large box open on a sideboard, Serge Ivanov said in the calmest imaginable high-pitched voice: "We were just talking about the bomb thrown yesterday in the Grand Theater. None of us knows any more than the newspapers have reported. Do either of you know anything else?"

"Nothing," said Grigoryi. "The action of a loner, an independent individual, probably simple-minded— according to the press, the bomb, although it would have been terribly destructive if it had exploded, seems to have been put together by an inexperienced child."

"That didn't prevent the child, simple-minded as he may be, from running away, escaping and going into hiding…and the police having no suspicion of where he might be. No one knows whether he's tall or short, young or old. He's certainly an individual, and a loner— but to have been able to remain unknown before, during and after his exploit, the brother can't be simple-minded!" These words had been spoken, not without irony, by the old lady, who was utterly bourgeois in appearance, wore ordinary spectacles and had her fine white hair gathered into two bandeaux.

With a hint of respect, Grigoryi said: "My dear Helena, I'm only speaking as a chemist."

"Yes, yes," said the old lady, smiling. "And I wanted to tease you a little, Grigoryi—but I'd really be quite astonished if, even though he's a mediocre student of elementary chemistry, the author of yesterday's exploit were devoid of intelligence, or at least cunning."

Grigoryi also smiled broadly. Then he made a gesture that commanded attention, and said in a grave tone: "Comrades, there's something other than this inexpert and anonymous gesture that Katia and I have to bring to your attention today. It concerns the matter of Radiant Z, and I…"

Once again, however, the proverb that says "When you mention the wolf, look out—he'll be there!" was abruptly verified. They had been talking about the "author of yesterday's exploit" for an hour—and, in fact, talking about nothing else. At the very moment when Grigoryi directed their thoughts toward another subject, although they had not yet turned to it, he was interrupted by the opening of the door and the entrance of an individual at the sight of whom the entire company rose to its feet, including the respectable old lady.

And Doctor Ivanov hurried forward, both arms extended. "Oh, what a nice surprise, my dear Maître! I certainly don't intend any reproach, but we see you so rarely because of your work, which is so admirable and so useful to the great and sacred cause of world emancipation…"

It was in such terms, even in congratulating one another, that the leaders of international espionage and universal Anarchism, hid their formidable and pitiless desire, their egotistical thirst for power and domination, their monstrous pride, and their furious humiliation at not already being among the masters of the world. In reality, they wanted, not the world's emancipation—for thus employed, the word signifies nothing—but rather its submission to their own ideas and their personal tyranny.

The man to whom Doctor Serge Ivanov had spoken with such admiring respect and such "bourgeois" reverence was the illustrious professor Alexis Roudine—who said, after shaking everyone's hand: "But I'm not alone, and I assure you that a humble scientist like me isn't much by comparison with a child who will be the purest and most magnificent hero of our holy Cause!"

He stepped to one side, turned round, and made a gesture of introduction. Only then did they notice that he had, indeed, not come in alone, and they saw a young man with large yellow-tinted spectacles and a sickly face, but of considerable stature, to whom the Professor pointed, saying: "My dear Helena Gruss, my dear Ivanov, and you, beautiful Katia, Comrades, take a bow, for by virtue of the potential that he has, even more than what he has already tried to do, this young man is worthy of your respect.

"Adrien Fortis, who threw a bomb yesterday at the Grand Theater capable of killing or wounding two hundred people..."

# Part Three: The Artificial Heart

## *Chapter I: In the Bear's Jaws*

Eight hours later, Adrien Fortis was no longer ignorant regarding the organization of Espionage and Anarchism, and the preparations for war and nihilist action of which Serge Ivanov was the secret executive leader and of which Alexis Roudine constituted the sole archivist-historian, the supreme counselor, the inspirer, the financial backer and the frequent publisher of journals, tracts, pamphlets and books of propaganda—brutal, primitive and immediate propaganda, or savant, disguised and long-range, according to the case in point.

In fact, Adrien Fortis had played his part admirably.

Yes, played his part, for—haven't you guessed?—Adrien Fortis was, in reality, Leo Saint-Clair, the Nyctalope!

Eventually—and in what terribly tragic, tortuous and abominably mortal circumstances!—he would record the story of the rapid stages of his transformation and the prodigiously intelligent, courageous and self-confident deeds that he conceived and accomplished during this brief period of his life.[9] On Wednesday March

---

[9] La Hire inserts a footnote here: "It is the shorthand record of this story, scribbled on the right-hand pages of a vulgar notebook, that we have been able to receive in communication, thanks to which this chronicle of the Nyctalope's first exploits has been written. Several pages of the notebook were stained

20, 1912, however, at exactly 3:20 a.m., Leo Saint-Clair related nothing, because he had no time. The moment of the supreme action was very close at hand, and he had wanted to see—merely to see—and embrace his friends before hurling himself, coolly but recklessly, into that "supreme action," which would, in his opinion either give him victory or precipitate him into torture followed by death.

Every night during that long, interminable and exceedingly painful week, Robert Champeau, René Croqui and Jean Degains had waited for Leo Saint-Clair behind a little iron door, normally unused, which cut out a hollow rectangle in the least visible section of the high wall encircling the private Sanatorium du Bouchet.

That door opened into an alley that was always deserted by night, along which no one passed even by day but occasional servants from the neighboring villas desirous of taking a short cut.

Every night, from three until 3:30 a.m., all three of them grimly undertook that duty, although they would have been able to take turns. Since the morning of Wednesday March 13, Champeau, Croqui and Degains had been there, motionless and silent, behind that gate, waiting for their leader, whom they admired more every day, and who was now beloved with an increasingly-painful disquiet. Seven times the 30 minutes of waiting, initially vibrant with hope, then tremulous with anxiety, had run by without the cry of recognition that would bid

in blood." Readers who consider it perverse of La Hire to leave the heart of his story untold in this casual fashion might feel that a footnote informing them that he has a document in his possession that would have done the job, but that he has no intention of sharing it, is adding insult to injury.

them to open the door as quickly as possible resounding in the nocturnal silence.

Seven nights! What anguish!

A week without the slightest news, without a single telephone call, telegram, letter or note—which Monsieur Ambroise Dorsang would have been able to receive discreetly and would have immediately passed on.

Finally, at 3:17 a.m. on March 20, the cry had rent the air. The door was opened; the Nyctalope came in; the door was closed again. They ran into the garden.

"No, no, I won't explain anything!" said the Nyctalope to Champeau, Croqui and Degains—who, shivering with emotion, stood elbow-to-elbow in front of him in the vestibule of the private chalet put at the disposal of the "French forwards" in the Sanatorium grounds. With a fraternal ardor he embraced them forcefully one after another, and continued rapidly and incisively: "In an hour, I'll have won or lost! I've come to tell you and embrace you. And I'm leaving again!"

Champeau seized him violently by the shoulders. "Give us something to do!" he cried. "There's mortal danger, isn't there?—I sense it. Tell me."

"Yes," said Leo, subjugated momentarily by the force of that anguished affection.

"Then we're going with you."

"Yes, yes, all together!" cried Degains and Croqui, excitedly.

But the Chief got hold of himself again. "No! I'm going alone. I have to be alone. The action is such that I can't pull it off unless I'm alone."

"But why?" they exclaimed, taking his hands and squeezing them.

"Come on, let me go—I don't have the time to explain."

It was true. He did not have the time, for the explanations would have been very difficult and quite long.

Could he actually have given them an explanation of his conduct, though? Rather than following the directives of a coolly-formulated plan, was he not following the lures of passion—of the first passion, the first love of his life—through a dark forest, within which his mind was fortunately tracing a logical path? Could he have confided to his three friends that he loved Aurora Malianova? Could he have explained to them that he had very quickly discovered that she was playing a dual role, that she was "the beautiful nihilist Katia," and that she was the lover, more by virtue of docility than amorousness, of the formidable Grigoryi, subject to his command and his will? Could he have confessed to them that, in spite of all of that, and perhaps because of it, he, Leo Saint-Clair, felt his love for Aurora-Katia growing to the point of irresistibility. And finally, could he have said to them:

"Yes, I love her, but I haven't forgotten my mission and my duty. On the contrary, I shall render my mission even more triumphant by extracting Aurora Malianova from the criminal milieu into which some unknown misfortune has hurled her. I shall get back the documents and the models, and I shall also save a young woman, the young woman I love…"

Ah, like all the young people of his era. Leo Saint-Clair had read the overly generous and Utopian *Resurrection* by Tolstoy, and he was sincere—just as sincere as the young men long before his time who had committed suicide after reading *Werther*![10]

---

[10] Leo Tolstoy's *Resurrection* (1899) was the author's last novel, and was so eagerly expected that it rapidly outsold *Anna Karenina* and *War and Peace*. Many readers were, how-

"Come on! Come on!" he repeated, detaching himself forcefully and skillfully from his friends' clenched hands. "Calm down, damn it!" And he burst out laughing. He had the strength to laugh.

That physical serenity had more effect than any words on the nerves of Champeau, Croqui and Degains. The three "forwards," subdued and disciplined, stood back from their Chief.

Then, very calmly, Saint-Clair said: "At 5 a.m., I must finish the final act. I've made arrangements to ensure that, at that time, no man will be in the house where the documents and apparatus are to be found."

He was not telling the whole truth, although he was not lying; there would indeed, be "no man" in the house, but only a woman: Katia! After a brief pause he continued: "Listen to me carefully! If I haven't returned by seven o'clock, or rather, if I haven't telephoned Profes-

---

ever, bitterly disappointed—and not a few annoyed—by its harrowing indictment of human justice and exploitation, as discovered by its hero, a penitent nobleman who visits the maid he once ruined in Siberia after she is wrongly convicted of murder. It is not at all obvious how reading *Resurrection* could have given birth to Saint-Clair's dreams of "saving" Aurora from the attractions of radical politics, rather than making him want to join her. The young hero of J. W. Goethe's quasi-autobiographical novel *The Sorrows of Young Werther* (1774) commits suicide as a consequence of unrequited love, and the novel really does seem to have encouraged some of its more impressionable readers to follow suit. Perhaps, in view of Saint-Clair's reckless stupidity and blatant dereliction of duty in not telling his companions what they need to know—which would have allowed the entire affair to be tidied up without further ado—the latter was the book that had actually made the deeper impression on him.

sor Dorsang, warn General Breuil immediately and go with the police to number 18, Rue du Fossé in the Rive neighborhood. That's it!"

"18, Rue du Fossé, Rive neighborhood," Champeau repeated.

"Yes—now let's embrace. And *au revoir*...or *adieu!*"

He had dry eyes himself, but those of his three good companions were shining with tears.

"Shall we go as far as the little door with you?" asked Degains, timidly.

"Yes, to open and close it for me."

In his haste, though, and also because he was a Nyctalope, he got ahead of them and had to wait for them at the foot of the wall, for in their confusion they did not immediately think of making use of their pocket electric torches to dissipate the darkness in front of them. He welcomed them, laughing, and they were reassured by hearing him say, in his most serene voice: "Oh, my friends, it's quite something to be able to see clearly in the darkness. Open up, Robert! Light up, you others!"

Champeau opened the little door, which key had remained in his hand throughout the brief and pathetic encounter. Saint-Clair embraced his three friends yet again, rapidly and almost brutally—and then, launching himself into the alley, the Nyctalope disappeared.

Half an hour later, with the little key that Katia Malianova had confided that same day to the young man who represented himself as the anarchist Adrien Fortis, Leo Saint-Clair went into the house with the low porch in the Rue du Fossé that bore the number 18.

On the first floor, he knocked on the door in the appropriate manner, and was welcomed into Grigoryi's "studio," as he had expected, by the beautiful Katia, her friend Grigoryi being otherwise occupied that night.

Although Saint-Clair knew, however, that on the still-nocturnal morning of March 20, he would be alone for a few hours with the young woman he loved, and to whom he was finally going to talk with all his generous passion before recovering the documents and apparatus relating to Radiant Z—which he knew to be hidden in the laboratory adjoining the studio—he was far from anticipating that his entire plan would be wrecked as soon as the first words were spoken.

His quick and keen mind had a very clear conception of that violent, instantaneous upset as soon as his ears heard and his brain registered the words with which the young woman greeted him; "Good day! But is it still Adrien Fortis, or is it not rather Leo Saint-Clair that I now have before me?"

A thunderbolt!

Yes, but thunderbolts are not always fatal, when their lightning strikes three paces ahead of you!

Momentarily shaken, mentally and even physically, the Nyctalope collected himself and stood up straight, powerful by virtue of the self-control that was the principal characteristic of his personality, which was already completely formed.

He repressed the sudden constriction of his throat with a deep breath and pronounced, in an almost normal voice: "Ah, Katia, you've found me out…or rather, Aurora, you've recognized me! Be a good sport all round and tell me what it was that allowed you to recognize me."

Cold and tense, with her gaze insolent and challenging, she did not hesitate to reply: "Your eyes!"

"My eyes! Oh, but with my spectacles, that I've kept on almost all the time, and my reddened and swollen eyebrows..."

She shrugged her shoulders and continued, sardonically: "I only needed 20 seconds, the day before yesterday, in the evening. Twenty seconds during which, while you were sitting in the corner over there, you wiped the lenses of your spectacles while looking at me. Yes, you were looking at me—and you were no longer thinking about the mortal peril you had been running for a week. You were thinking about that moment in the garden of the clinic when you had looked at me for the first time in daylight, looked at me and seen me... Your eyes, the day before yesterday, had the same expression they had then. That was how I recognized you—for what is unmistakable is a loving gaze. Now, at that moment, as soon your eyes were reborn to the light of the Sun, you fell in love with me, Leo Saint-Clair! And it was the same loving gaze that, for twenty seconds in the evening of the day before yesterday, your eyes held for me..."

She breathed in. There was a sort of rapid palpitation in her breast, and she spat out, hoarsely: "And then my hatred recognized you!"

He shuddered, took a step backwards, made a naïve gesture, both hands reaching forwards, and stammered: "Your hatred! Your hatred?"

His face had become livid—and because of the artificial eruptions and scaly patches that made him ugly, that face would have been frightful and horrible if the fire of a sublime passion had not immediately animated, transformed and idealized it.

Leo Saint-Clair had only taken a single backward step; he took three forwards, then four, and put his arms on the young woman's shoulders. She tried instinctively to escape, but was vigorously restrained.

"Your hatred!" he said, again, but this time in a very soft voice, as if alive with nothing but love. "Can you hate me, Aurora? Why? Me, who loves you and want to save you—yes, save you! To tear you away from the sinister error into which you've been thrown—and I know by whom...for I have been told the story of Mademoiselle Katia Irenovna Malianova. You have run away from parents who love you, and an aristocratic social milieu in which you would normally have taken your place—a destiny in which nothing was lacking to make you happy...

"All that you have fled, and in such a manner that your bridges were burned behind you! You've listened to the cunning counsel, and then submitted to the brutal constraint, of a man who, by courtesy of an incident in which you only demonstrated an adorable weakness, took possession of you, body and soul...

"Katia! You are, for me, Aurora: the dawn, the light, and the revelation of love in the joy of the sun's glare! You are Aurora, and I deny everything that was in your life before the moment when I saw you in the clear morning light! I love you, Aurora! Let's go away together, not looking behind us. Let's go! And my love will be so great, so all-encompassing, so penetrating and so strong that it will animate you too...and you will love me!"

He was a child, who believed that love is contagious! He was a child, who, in his pure and radiant youth, saw nothing of that young woman but the face of a Madonna, and believed that her soul was made in the image of that beauty! He was a child, yes, who had wept with generous and compassionate emotion on reading the sentimental social dreams of Tolstoy! Before real life had formed him, he saw life through the lenses of utopian literature.

At the very moment when they were affirmed, however, his first and overly juvenile illusions were to receive the blow that would destroy them.

"Aurora...you will love me!"

She burst out laughing then, briefly contorted her entire body, escaped from of Saint-Clair's grasp like a slithering viper and ran to the far side of the studio, in the light of half-veiled electric lamps, sowing the air, which was heavy with tobacco fumes, with her laughter of bravado and shameless mockery: her frightful, infernal laughter. And that laughter broke Leo Saint-Clair's heart—actually broke it, as if the cruel woman had sunk her sharp fingernails into his naked, quivering and bloody viscera, and raked them...

He became unsteady, his eyes burning with sudden tears.

But a cry made him straighten up, and rendered his eyes dry, his heart pain-free and calm, and his brain lucid and cold.

That cry sprang from Katia's convulsed mouth: "Grigoryi! Grigoryi!"

It was no longer Leo Saint-Clair, tenderized by his first love and tortured by his first suffering, who made the prompt gesture, but the Nyctalope, in combat with the enemy.

What gesture? Right hand in pocket, arm extended, Browning leveled. And from the same lips that had trembled with words of love, and imperative command sprang forth: "Hands up!"

Instead of obeying, the man—the colossus—who was placidly coming into the studio from the next room came forward with his hands half-raised: enormous hands, open like claws about to seize their prey.

Moved by the instinct of self-preservation, his determination to defend himself and carry out his intended action, Leo Saint-Clair fired. He pressed the trigger of his weapon twice…

He understood immediately. Instead of the detonation of cartridges stuffed with powder and charged with bullets, the Browning only emitted two feeble clicks. *Yesterday afternoon*, he thought, *during my siesta, the real cartridges were replaced by blanks.*

Determined to fight anyway, he stepped back abruptly, raised his right arm, and hurled the steel Browning into Grigoryi's face with all his might.

The colossus had a hard skull, alas. The butt of the improvised projectile struck him on the forehead, and tore away a little flesh, causing blood to flow, but the progress of the Herculean body was neither stopped nor even slowed down.

Disarmed, relatively weak despite his vigor by comparison with his tall, broad and heavy adversary, Leo Saint-Clair was only able to fight for less than a minute. He was seized and bent backwards; his arms were twisted and pinned against his back; he found himself thrown face-down on to the carpet, where a heavy knee maintained him while agile fingers passed a cord around his joined wrists, wound it tightly and knotted it.

"Now, comrade, get up. You won't come to any harm, at least for the moment—nor later, if you're a little cooperative… Good! Sit down, my friend—we need to have a chat."

Grigoryi had said this while Saint-Clair, with a supple thrust of the hips, had turned over on the carpet, then got to his knees and stood up. After pausing to draw breath, he ended up sitting down in a leather armchair.

His spectacles had fallen off during the struggle. Now exposed, his keen, ardent eyes, deliberately half-closed, darted a sharp gaze between eyelids almost bloodied by blepharitis, artificially created and actively maintained. That gaze went initially to Katia, motionless and mute in the shadows at the back of the room, then to Grigoryi—who sat down heavily on a stool, wiping his bloody forehead and nose with a section of his handkerchief.

The Russian made a bandage of the same handkerchief, which he wrapped around his forehead, and which Katia came spontaneously to knot at the back of his head. When that was done, the young woman retreated again into an ill-lit corner, as if to signify that she was not going to involve herself in the discussion.

"Yes," Grigoryi resumed, in his slow, deep voice, "we need to have a chat, Saint-Clair. You're a bold fellow, and you have my esteem. Without Katia's perspicacity, you would have turned us over and defeated us without even having to fight us." He laughed briefly, and continued with sly mockery: "Let that be a lesson to you, my lad. When you next fall in love... if you live any longer than 24 hours... well, don't put your love into your gaze. Katyushka caught sight of it—that's what betrayed you. Silly boy!"

He shrugged his shoulders. Then, in a different tone, which was heavy, emphatic and menacing, he went on: "But it isn't about that any more. Forget your disappointed passion, my lad, and think about conducting yourself in such a manner that you can catch up, in the matter of love affairs, in the course of the rest of your life, which has only just started. No, it isn't about that,

Leo Saint-Clair, but the invention made by your father, the electrician and chemist. You understand?"

During this flow of words, making a triple effort, Leo Saint-Clair had recovered all of him calmness, all of his self-composure and all of his courageous, sagacious and prudent lucidity. It was in his normal voice that he said: "I understand. I've been listening to you and your accomplices for a week, in order to discover what my father didn't tell me—or, in his mental confusion, didn't think to tell me. Something essential is missing from the documents and the scale models of that apparatus, which prevents you from being able to utilize the invention and construct complete working models. Is that it?"

"Yes," said Grigoryi, resentfully.

"So what?" Saint-Clair queried.

"So," the other resumed, "you'll tell me what you know—for you worked with your father. He directed you in studies that were in concordance with his science and the applications he made of it, or wanted to make of it. You must know the nature, composition and usage of the essential element that is missing from the documents and the models we have in our possession. You're going to tell us about it."

"No."

"What?"

"No."

The two negations had been pronounced in a defiant and decisive tone, but without any fervent anger, expressing a decision coldly made and final.

Grigoryi closed his enormous hands and his entire face underwent a brutal nervous contraction. He thumped his own thighs with his fists. Brutally, he said: "You'll talk! You'll tell us everything you know! I'll give you 24 hours, and not one more. Tomorrow, at daybreak, if you still haven't talked and refuse again, I'll submit you to torture...to a torture that will draw you gradually closer to death. You have 24 hours to reflect and capitulate before suffering. As soon as dawn breaks tomorrow, you'll start to find out what torture by fire is like, then those of hunger and thirst..."

He got up, started pacing back and forth like a caged bear, then stopped in front of Katia—who had remained still and silent in the dark corner—and pronounced slowly, in French, with extreme gentleness: "Katyushka, my darling, go into the kitchen and make us some coffee. Don't worry about anything else. When you've finished and had breakfast with us, you'll leave and go back to the clinic. Listen to me carefully, Katyushka, and obey me as you love me..."

"I'm listening, Grigoryi, and I'll obey you," murmured the young woman, humble and smiling.

"You'll go back to your clinic...and you won't budge for a week. Watch, observe, listen to anything that might be said over there about this fellow and his three absent friends. If you learn anything, and when you're certain that you won't be caught, telephone Monsieur Roudine, in Russian. Vassily will act as messenger between him and me. But whatever you find out, and whatever happens in the field of your observation, don't leave Lausanne—don't even go out of the clinic for a week. In a week, this business will be over, whether this fellow has been sent back to France by us, defeated, or whether his cadaver, weighed down by scrap iron, is rotting at the bottom of Lake Leman. Come on, Katyushka—the coffee...and then you have to go."

"Yes, my darling."

The young woman emerged from the shadowed corner, passed in front of Saint-Clair in the full glare of the light without glancing at him, and disappeared through a little glazed door at the other side of the studio, which opened into a sort of vestibule beyond which was a fairly large room leading to the kitchen and dining-room.

Grigoryi stretched himself out on the divan and lit a cigarette, which he smoked slowly, his eyes fixed on the low ceiling.

In the armchair where he was still seated, with his hands tied behind his back, holding his upper body upright and his head high, Leo Saint-Clair remained calm and attentive. He was frowning slightly, and from time to time he bit into his lower lip with is incisors. He did not modify his attitude when Katia Malianova brought a tray, which she deposited on the table. The tray bore a coffee-pot, three cups, toast, butter, jam, sugar, spoons and dessert-knives.

"Saint-Clair," said Grigoryi, getting to his feet, "I'm going to untie you so that you can eat more comfortably—but don't do anything stupid, hey? Firstly, these knives are only sharp enough to cut butter, and secondly, I have my eye on you. One suspicious move on your part, and I'll knock you out with one punch. Oh, only to stun you, not to kill you. For during 24four hours without touching you, then six or seven days of torturing you in various ways, I'd rather hear you talk and let you save your life. On the evening of the sixth or seventh day, though, if you end up dying, it will be your own fault, for that will prove that you've been crazy enough to keep quiet."

And with consummate skill, he removed the cord from his prisoner's wrists.

Leo Saint-Clair was hungry. He ate and drank comfortably, without any apparent emotion. He often looked at Katia, but the young woman did not meet his eyes once.

When the silent breakfast was over, the young woman took the tray away, came back to tidy up the corner of the table, and then vanished into the kitchen for the last time. She only showed herself again to put on her hat, gloves and mantle.

"Don't forget your handbag," said Grigoryi.

She picked it up and stood on tiptoe to offer her lips, on which he colossus planted a kiss—but without taking his eyes off Leo Saint-Clair, who was sitting in the armchair, with his free hands still resting on the edge of the table.

And Katia Malianova went out, without having glanced at the noble fellow who, thanks to her, was now in the jaws of the bear.

## Chapter II: Torture? Murder?

When the young woman had gone, Grigoryi came back to sit down on the divan facing Saint-Clair, and he said:

"My boy, you must often have laughed at us secretly in the last week. We were completely taken in by the sham of your physical disfigurement, which I now understand to have been produced by some medico-surgical intervention. We also believed in your doubtless-invented family misfortunes, and had no suspicions regarding the bomb you threw in the theater, although I understand now that the whole business was organized by you and your friends with the Geneva police. You were even lucky that Vassily, who happened to be in the audience, ran after you, caught up with you and, thinking that he was saving you, took you straight to the intellectual center of our organization—which is to say, Monsieur Roudine's house. It's our strength, but also our weakness, never to check up on the antecedents of men who come to us and immediately inspire our trust."

He shook his head, took a cigarette, lit it, and took three draughts upon it, then went on, his voice a trifle heavy: "Oh, I know full well that if Vassily hadn't been there, you'd have succeeded in insinuating yourself among us, thanks to that trick with the bomb and the clues the police had given you about the cafés, restaurants and other places where exiled Russians—almost all of them nihilists—hung out, along with pro-German spies many of whom are Russian...and you would have attained your ends, if Katia..."

He interrupted himself again, smoked a little, then said, in a confident tone: "Katia you see, is incomparably useful to us, because she knows how to make everyone love her, while she only loves me."

These unexpected words made Leo Saint-Clair shiver, as he felt a dull pain in his heart—but he clenched his teeth in order not to let any exclamation of his indignation, pain and hatred escape.

Grigoryi was, in any case, continuing. "She's intelligent, refined and clever, my Katyushka. She has a prodigious memory. She never forgets the expression of a gaze, the sound of a word, the direction of the most furtive gesture. For your debut in life and love, my lad, you had to play a hand that was too difficult, and you lost the game. For you, now, it's a matter of paying the price."

Just then, for the first time since he had fallen into the trap, the Nyctalope saw a ray of light in the menacing darkness of his situation. He recalled that, before leaving his friends at 3:30 that morning, he had issued this instruction: "Listen to me carefully! If I haven't returned by 7 a.m., or rather, if I haven't telephoned Professor Dorsang, warn General Breuil immediately and go with the police to number 18, Rue du Fossé in the Rive neighborhood. That's it!" And his ears clearly heard Champeau's firm voice repeating: "18, Rue du Fossé, Rive neighborhood."

Then, forgetting everything that the colossus Grigoryi had just said, Leo Saint-Clair had a smile on his lips and a gleam of confident hope in his eyes. His eyes immediately went to check the clock conventionally set between two flower-vases on the mantelpiece of the studio—and he saw that the hands stood at 6:43 a.m.

*In about 17 minutes*, he thought, *my three friends will alert the General. At 7:30 at the latest, the secret police will be alerted. At 8 a.m., I'll be free.*

And as Grigoryi had not retied his hands, Saint-Clair lifted his right hand, extended it toward the other and said, casually: "Would you care to give me a cigarette?"

"Willingly, but not immediately," the Russian replied, "for I still have a few words to say to you and something to show you. Afterwards, you may smoke as much as you want; a full box of cigarettes will be placed at your disposal."

He got up. Visibly ready to fight, with his fists clenched and his body slightly inclined toward the still-seated Saint-Clair, he said: "You know that my laboratory is here. Precious! You'll certainly understand that from the very start, when it was first installed in this house, we've worked to put it as far as possible out of the reach of the police. Good!

"You've learned many things about us, but not those which constitute our real secrets, which are only known to five or six men in the world, and only one woman—Katia. You shall now see one of those secrets with your own eyes…"

As Saint-Clair made as if to get up, however, the colossus said: "No, not yet. Let me finish speaking. Now that you've been unmasked, I suspect that you must have remained in contact with your friends, perhaps with the police…in fact, I'm sure of it. And I think you must have told your friends that if, at some appointed time, they haven't heard from you, then it's in this house that you'll be found, alive or dead. Hey—don't move or I'll hit you!"

Tense, with all his muscles taught, Leo Saint-Clair suppressed the instinctive movement that impelled him once again to get to his feet. And Grigoryi continued, with heavy sarcasm: "My dear beautiful Katia has taught me to observe a physiognomy, to interpret a smile or a grimace, to follow the direction and understand the significance of a glance. A few moments ago, my boy, you smiled and looked at the clock. Eh? I've guessed it! No need for us to explain further. Well, as Dante wrote, and I'll translate in case you don't understand Italian: "Abandon all hope ye who enter here." Yes, you shall see— for I've almost finished speaking, and I'll show you the thing. Get up!"

His heart gripped by an anguished curiosity, Leo got up.

"Walk toward the door, open it, go out and go down to the bottom of the staircase—and don't forget that I'm at your heels and can knock you down with a single blow of my fist. Don't bother to cry out; even someone listening expressly, in the street, wouldn't hear the most desperate and panic-stricken howls. The walls of this old building are very thick, and you'll see... March!"

Saint-Clair obeyed. While he opened the door to the landing he did not see what Grigoryi was doing behind him. He did not see Grigoryi put his open hand into a sort of cranny between two thick volumes on a bookshelf, so that his entire forearm disappeared therein, operate a turning movement through a quarter-circle in two opposite directions, one after another, and then withdraw his arm and hand—after which the two stout volumes came together again.

Although Saint-Clair did not see that, he did hear a noise—an unfamiliar noise, which did not capture his attention and which he did not "realize" and understand until a few minutes later.

He was on the landing, which was feebly lit by an electric bulb suspended from a wire.

"Go down to the bottom of the staircase," Grigoryi repeated.

The young man continued to obey. At the bottom of the staircase, however, which was illuminated by a second bulb, he stopped, suddenly stupefied.

Twenty times in the last week he had passed that way, coming from the street or going to it. He knew that there was a direct and free route from the staircase along the corridor terminated by the deep porch, without any obstacle of any sort. For someone entering, the open stairway was a continuation of the corridor; for someone leaving, the corridor extended the stairway horizontally. Now, having reached the bottom of the staircase, Leo Saint-Clair was no longer confronted by the corridor, but by a wall. A wall! A wall that blocked the stairway completely, from left to right and top to bottom. A wall that made the bottom of he stairway into a cul-de-sac with no exit or gap.

"Oh!" he exclaimed, dully.

Behind him, Grigoryi burst out laughing.

Shivering, Saint-Clair turned round.

He saw Grigoryi back up against the wall and heard him say: "You see, my lad? Good. Go past me and climb back up—let's go back to the studio. You'll see something else, in the laboratory and the kitchen too. Afterwards, I'll explain. Come on, be brave! Up you go!"

Bravely containing his emotion, and beginning to work it out, to understand, Saint-Clair obeyed again.

In the studio, the laboratory and he kitchen, Grigoryi instructed him to open the casements of the windows, which he did. As he expected, instead of empty space, in which he should have been able to open and the shutters, now non-existent, there was a wall!

"Well, Monsieur the son of the engineer Pierre Saint-Clair," said Grigoryi, "that's nice work, as they say in France. It's me, Grigoryi the architect and tech-nologist, who contrived that. Ordinarily, downstairs and up here, those walls, build inside steel frames, are hidden in the thickness of the old walls of the house. In times of danger, they come out of their hiding-places. And where visitors would have seen a staircase in the corridor, or three ordinary windows by looking up from the cour-tyard...they only see the wall, so carefully made up and stained, maintained in a superficial decrepitude, that the movable plates are indistinguishable from the thick walls of the old house. You understand now eh?"

Saint-Clair was facing him now. Sniggering, the co-lossus repeated: "You understand? Your friends or the police, or the police and your friends, will be able to come to number 18, Rue du Fossé, which you must have indicated to them, with that laudable precision of mind that I've noticed. At the end of the corridor, as you can imagine, they won't bang on the wall. They'll knock on the door to the right, which you must have noticed. That door will open, and they'll find themselves in the pres-ence of an old maidservant, who will introduce them to her mistress, an old lady with spectacles and bandeaux, very respectable, whom you've met in Doctor Ivanov's house and heard called Helena, but who is better known in Geneva as Olga Cheminska, a doctor of medicine, the worthy patroness of several charitable endeavors, holder of a gold medal earned during epidemics, etc. etc. And if your friends and the policemen visit the whole house, if they even go into the interior courtyard, they'll see nothing but the least suspicious of walls, the most ordinary of roofs, while the venerable Doctor Olga Cheminska will say to them: 'You must have got the wrong address…' Well, young Nyctalope, isn't that nicely put together? And aren't you admirably served for the commencement of your life of adventures? For you were born under the sign of Adventure, and you'll have a very interesting life…if you get out of here safe and sound!"

The last part of the sentence was pronounced in such a tone that Leo Saint-Clair immediately forgot about everything he had just seen and heard, in order to concentrate on his own plight.

*That's true*, he said to himself. *That's true! If I get out of here safe and sound…I can no longer count on anyone else. I'm alone. Speak or die! We shall see!*

Gathering all the strength of his inner being in order to master his nerves, command his muscles and control the beating of his heart and the circulation of his blood, the son of the engineer Pierre Saint-Clair, facing the enemy, said in the calmest possible tone; "Would you care to give me a cigarette?"

Grigoryi Alexandrovich was amazed, but he soon collected himself, and assumed a most ambiguous expression to sway: "Well, Leo Saint-Clair, you've got guts. It's a great pity that you're not with us but against us. Yes, you could be one of the great leaders of the impending world revolution, in spite of your youth. But it'll only go all the harder with you, and I play a tight game. I've got all the trumps in my hand, to be sure, and…"

"No you haven't," the Nyctalope put in.

"What?"

"No—you haven't got the secret of Radiant Z."

Grigoryi clenched his fists and growled: "I'll get it."

"You shan't!"

"I'll kill you."

"So be it! In the meantime, give me that box of cigarettes that you promised me. And as you've also promised me 24 hours, leave me in peace!"

When he is naturally endowed with courage and endurance, with solid physical health, a young man is incapable of despair; he braves all suffering, and death appears to him to be impossible. If, in addition, he is animated by the sentiment of a grave duty, he is rich in every interior strength and capable of any heroism. These are excellent dispositions for fighting the enemy and forcing victory, or for finally accepting the death in which one did not believe, rather than deeming it a disaster by which one is horrified.

Thus was Leo Saint-Clair, the Nyctalope, throughout the day of Wednesday March 20.

In anticipation of the total and hermetic imprisonment to which events might consign him, Grigoryi always had significant reserves of canned food in his sealed apartment. There was an inexhaustible supply of drinking-water from the tap in the kitchen. As for the necessary ventilation, it was delivered by the air currents that could be established between the hearths of the studio-bedroom, the kitchen and the laboratory by opening the interior doors. In consequence, the state of absolute imprisonment could be maintained for at least a fortnight. This time, Grigoryi estimated that if he had not obtained any information from his captive within a week, he never would obtain any, and the captivity would end with the death of his prisoner.

As for the principle of respect for human life, that was *nothing* to the nihilist Grigoryi Alexandrovich. If the occasion arose, he would unhesitatingly give the last drop of his blood and the last breath in his body for his furiously fanatical cause; he had no scruples at all about taking anyone else's life.

As for Saint-Clair, he thought that the first condition of possible salvation was to remain lucid in mind and sturdy in body. He smoked very little, and drank moderately of the wine—which was quite good—that Grigoryi offered him with two meals, and he ate in a manner appropriate to his hunger, which was normal. As he had not slept for a single moment the previous night, he gladly accepted the divan that Grigoryi yielded to him, contenting himself with two armchairs pushed together facing one another, extended by a pouf set between them.

The captive slept profoundly, but the jailer slept with one eye and one ear open; he was accustomed to it, and the slightest sound or displacement of air within the room would have woken him up instantly and put him on the defensive, ready for an attack. The Nyctalope, however, had no thought of attempting an offensive action in which, without a weapon, he would immediately be placed in an inferior position. He needed sleep, so he slept—and he would probably have had "a lie-in," as they say, if he had not been woken up by a sharp impact on his left shoulder.

"Ow!" he said, sitting up.

He did not realize immediately where he was, or in what circumstances—but a harsh voice brought him round and reintegrated him into the situation at a stroke.

"Hey there, Leo Saint-Clair! On this Thursday March 21, sunrise is at 5:54 a.m. It's exactly 6 a.m. Stand up! The moment has come to choose."

The Nyctalope rubbed his eyes, which had initially been dazzled by the light of all the electric lamps illuminated in the studio. Then, clear-sighted and perfectly self-controlled, he stood up, looked the cruel-faced colossus straight in the face, although slightly from below because of the difference in their heights, and said: "Well, here I am."

The 24 hours of reflection have elapsed," growled Grigoryi. "You have to make a decision, my lad. I repeat the alternatives: either you give me all the technical information necessary to the practical construction and setting up of Radiant Z, or I'll start submitting you, in five minutes, to the triple torture of fire, thirst and hunger."

Leo Saint-Clair went pale, to the point of becoming livid, for all his blood flowed to his heart, which almost burst, and was extremely painful for a few seconds. Then a long and violent shiver ran through him. Immediately afterwards, the color flowed back into his cheeks and his eyes sparkled. He slowly folded his arms, and more slowly still he said, in a firm voice: "If you are an executioner, Grigoryi Alexandrovich, do your work. Personally, I shall do my duty; I won't talk."

"Very well," said the Russian, furiously. And he slapped Saint-Clair full in the face. The latter, unready for that immediate brutality, had not steeled himself against it, and he fell to the floor on his side. Before he was able to tense his muscles, collect himself and get up—for he had only lost his balance and not his consciousness of everything—he was grabbed by Grigoryi, who put his arms behind him, brought his wrists together and clasped them in steel handcuffs, which he had ready to hand.

"Get up now," said the executioner. "Stay upright, sit down or lie down—it's all the same to me. Wherever you are and however you arrange yourself, you'll be subjected to torture. Listen and reply, if you have the courage. Did you notice, yesterday evening, that the soup made from concentrated stock tasted a little too strong and salty?"

Saint-Clair was standing up, leaning his back and his clenched fists on the edge of the massive table. He was panting slightly. "Yes, perhaps," he gasped.

"That was to make you thirsty. Personally, I'll drink a large glass of water before making my breakfast. You can watch me drink. Soon, my lad, you'll start to know what it is to be thirsty, to see a glass of clear water in front of you, and to hear the kitchen tap running, without being able to touch it…"

He disappeared through the glazed door to the kitchen, leaving it open, and he came back, holding up a glass of delightfully pure fresh water, making it sparkle in the electric light. Slowly, spacing out his gulps, he drank it in front of his victim, who had become impassive again.

When the glass was empty, he put it on the mantelpiece. Then he lit a cigarette and…he suddenly jabbed the still-incandescent match into Saint-Clair's forehead.

"Ah!" howled the unfortunate, recoiling so violently with his entire body that he lay on his back on the table-top, as if broken in two.

Above him, Grigoryi's frightful leaning face wore a cruel mocking smile, and from the awful mouth of the sadistic torturer these words emerged, slightly deformed by the cigarette maintained in the corner of his lips: "The first caress of the fire, my lad! I'm going to take all your clothes off, and lay bare your neck, your arms, and your entire torso. You can run this way and that, but I'll always catch up with you. There are matches, there are the lighted ends of cigarettes and cigars, there are irons reddened by the flame of a blow-torch. The pain of the burns will augment your thirst, the thirst will give you a fever, which the hunger will bring down, but which will soon rise again, a torture in itself. Burned from moment to moment, panting with thirst, racked by hunger, shivering with fever but with a lucid mind—for I know how to measure out the torture—you'll go from day to night and from night to day…until you talk or die… There!"

And with a punch in the ribs, he sent the martyr sprawling on the carpet, where he grabbed him, turned him over, tore off his jacket and his short, and burned him in the hollow of his throat by stubbing out the lighted cigarette, which he had abruptly revived with a whistling breath.

## Chapter III: Jean Degains' Idea

The previous day, at 7 a.m, Robert Champeau, René Croqui and Jean Degains, in their chalet in the Sanatorium du Bouchet, had been standing in the middle of a little room austerely furnished as a study, around a table on which stood a telephone apparatus.

In the same room, a clock on the mantelpiece sounded its silvery chimes. After the seventh sonorous chime here was an extensive prolongation of subtle vibrations, and silence.

The three young men looked at one another, severe, sullen and anxious at the same time—and Robert Champeau said, duly: "Nothing. He hasn't come back. He hasn't telephoned Professor Dorsang, since we haven't heard the telephone ring."

"Let's ask the Professor," said Croqui.

"All right!" said Champeau. He picked up the transmitter. "Hello!"

It was Monsieur Dorsang himself who answered.

"Thank you, Monsieur," Champeau murmured—and he hung up, growling: "Nothing!"

"Alert the General, then," said Croqui.

"Of course!"

The consequences that second telephone call were immediate, and had a prompt sequel that proceeded without any interruption—which is to say that at 8 a.m. on the morning of Wednesday March 20, the Rue du Fossé in the Rive neighborhood of Geneva was invaded by 20 men who had arrived in a van that stopped outside number 18.

Under the deep porch, the door to the building was open. There was a young woman on the threshold who was just about to go out, with a milk-jug in one hand and a basket in the other. She was pushed back to the end of the corridor.

"Gentlemen, gentlemen! What's going on? What do you want?" she complained, in a strong Basle accent.

The men were now filling the corridor. One of them, followed by three young men, stopped in front of the maidservant, from whom the others were immediately separated, sent to form a cordon in the street, where two were stationed in front of the motionless van and two to either side of the door.

"Who are you? What's your name?"

The trembling maidservant replied volubly to the gentleman who was interrogating her, whom she guessed to be the one in charge of the others. "My name is Frieda Diegmann. I cook and keep house for Madame Doctor Olga Cheminska, who is well-known to everyone in the neighborhood."

"Very well! We'll see about that."

Looking around the rectangular cul-de-sac that formed the extremity of the corridor, the Commissaire only saw one door, to his right. It seemed respectably bourgeois. A well-polished copper plate was gleaming there, on which was engraved in old-fashioned black letters:

*MADAME OLGA CHEMINSKA*
*General Practitioner*

Also gleaming, equally well-polished, was a little copper square next to the doorpost, from which projected the button of an electric bell.

"My word," said the Commissaire. "I've never been here before, although this is my native neighborhood, but I know Doctor Cheminska by name." He was muttering in a very low voice, while looking at the three young men grouped closely around him. "Her reputation is excellent...a great philanthropist, and knowledgeable and charitable physician. Ahem! I'm rather afraid that there's been another mistake..." Lowering his voice even further, and lowering his head, he added in a confidential tone: "In these affairs of espionage and intrigue, one often comes across empty houses or false addresses. Are you quite certain, you three, that it's number 18, Rue du Fossé?"

In the same tone, and in unison, Champeau, Croqui and Degains replied: "Quite certain!"

"Ahem! Well, we shall see!" Turning back to the maidservant, who seemed to have recovered her tranquility, the Commissaire asked: "Is Madame the Doctor at home?"

"Yes, Monsieur."

"You have the key, of course."

"Yes, Monsieur."

"Well, open up and go tell Madame the Doctor that a Commissaire of the Special Police dealing with foreigners is obliged to speak to her without delay. I shall come in with you, and these three gentlemen too. Go on, open up!"

With a gesture, he invited the three young Frenchmen to follow him. The instructions they had received from high places less than half an hour earlier had imposed a duty on them that they were carrying out with good grace and sympathy.

As might have been expected after these preliminaries, however, Madame Doctor Cheminska exclaimed in astonishment, showed herself to be discreetly indignant, but yielded nevertheless to the request of the

Commissaire—who, she had to admit, was only doing his duty—and opened all the interior doors of her apartment. The visit had no result. Through one of the kitchen doors they gained access to a rather large courtyard with no other exit, surrounded by the blank walls of other low and dilapidated buildings, which, on investigation, did not offer anything suspicious. There was nothing in the old paved courtyard, between the paving-stones of which grass was growing, but a sort of drain-opening, with a movable trap-door, into which Madame Cheminska's maidservant threw household rubbish.

The Commissaire's investigations, aided by Champeau, Croqui and Degains, were scrupulous, since they lasted until midday. It was necessary to accept that Madame the Doctor was above suspicion and that nothing supported the belief that a den of nihilists and criminal spies was established at number 18, Rue du Fossé. On interrogation, the neighbors declared that Madame Cheminska received a great many visitors at all hours, but that they had never seen anything abnormal, suspicious or even particularly remarkable.

At 1 p.m., when Champeau, Croqui and Degains returned to their chalet in the Sanatorium, where Genera Le Breuil was waiting for them, they were in despair, although not all equally so. And the General, who shared a meal of cold meat and fruit brought from the Sanatorium by a trusted servant, observed throughout the meal that the face and attitude of Jean Degains differed noticeably from those of his companions. Champeau and Croqui were downcast and somber, while Degains was meditative and intense.

In the end, the General could bear it no longer. As they got up to go into the garden and stroll around it while talking over the situation, he clapped the young

Briard on the shoulder and said, in a paternally authoritative fashion: "Come on, my friend, you've thought of something your comrades haven't. What is it?"

On these words, Champeau and Croqui, who were walking in front, stopped and turned round. They saw Degains smile slightly, and heard him reply: "It's a question of chimneys, General."

"What?"

"What do you mean?"

"Have you got an idea?"

Degains shook his slender head, with its slightly superabundant red hair, and said, calmly: "Let's not go out yet, if you please. I need a table, some blank paper and a pencil. We've got all that in the study."

"Well, let's go in then," said the General.

Two minutes later, Le Breuil and the three youths were seated around the table in the study, from which Degains had removed the telephone apparatus in order to make more room. He spread out a large sheet of blank paper in front of him and, with his pencil in his hand, he set about making a line-drawing, and then another, and yet another—which were, in reality, architectural plans in elevation, in profile and in surface.

While drawing, he talked. "This is how numbers 16, 18 and 20, Rue du Fossé, presented themselves to us, with their facades connected to one another: the doors, the windows, the roofs. Good! I'm sure of my memory. When my eyes see something, there's a photograph in my brain...

"Look—here, on the roofs, are all the chimneys that I saw, counted and observed. This one and this one belong to house number 16, and these two to number 20. All right, nothing more to say. This other one, here, is the collective chimney of the two hearths that are in the doctor's apartment; again, nothing more to say. But do you see? There are three more chimneys here, in the very center, two of them narrow earthenware pipes, one very broad, built of stone. They must belong, without any possible doubt, to house number 18. Now, inside that house, we only saw the doctor's two hearths—hearths whose flues, coming together in the wall, have only one outlet on the roof.

"So, the question arises: to what are the three supplementary chimneys connected? And one conclusion imposes itself—one alone. House number 18 is deceptive. To the view of a police search, it only offers the doctor's apartment: living rooms on the ground floor, bedrooms on the first floor, attic store-rooms under the roof. All well and good. But what about the supplementary chimneys?"

He fell silent, and looked at General Le Breuil, Robert Champeau and René Croqui one after the other, all of whom were stupefied. Then, with a little smile at the corners of his mouth, he went on: "My father is an architect. I've learned from him that quite often, as a chance result of successive constructions, the layouts of houses can offer one or more optical illusions that, by virtue of lack of a distant standpoint or the impossibility of seeing the whole from a bird's eye view, prevent one from getting an exact, complete and detailed impression of the buildings, especially if one is inside them. The only thing that can reveal the trickery, if there is some trickery, is a study of the quantity and position of the chimneys, relative to the number of hearths in the building...

"So, when I saw that there were three chimneys too many on the roof, relative to the interior hearths and their flues, the idea occurred to me that number 18 was deceptive, and that the trickery concealed an apartment.

In consequence, that's where Saint-Clair is imprisoned. That's all."

"Good God!" cried Champeau. "Why didn't you say all that when we were out there with the police?"

"For two reasons," Degains replied, without hesitation. "The first is that all this wasn't very clear or definite in my mind. The second is that, since there's trickery, it might very well include a secret means of escape, through which the criminals would have fled, perhaps even being able to take Saint-Clair with them, if they hadn't killed him when the lady doctor, alerted by my revelations or by the Commissaire's new attitude, had discreetly sent some signal. For, despite all appearances, I believe that Madame Cheminska is an accomplice of the spies. She's cunning, of course—but when it comes to cunning, I'm as good as anyone, and I observed a gleam in the doctor's eyes the whole time. A little glimmer in their utmost depths, which made me think: *You're telling us tales, buxom lady, you're stringing us along and you're laughing inside.*" He thumped the table with his fist and got to his feet, saying, in a duly menacing tone: "But he who laughs last laughs longest."

Champeau, Croqui and the General had also risen to their feet, excitedly. The first-named cried, violently: "Let's go back there right away!"

"No," said Degains, with stubborn quietness. "No, old chap, we must have patience. Precipitate and ill-considered action might get Saint-Clair killed. In my opinion, *they* will be content to hold him to get more out of his father, who is known to have more inventions in his head than just Radiant Z. Saint-Clair is a prisoner. A few hours more won't aggravate the conditions of his captivity much more, but rather than risk being denounced by him—who must know a great deal about them by now—the bandits won't hesitate to kill him if the alarm is raised."

"What then?" sighed Croqui, tremulously.

"We use cunning, cunning and more cunning! Which doesn't exclude audacity—on the contrary; I therefore add: audacity, audacity, and more audacity! But if it's not completely dressed up beforehand in cunning, audacity might ruin everything!"

That was pure Jean Degains.

The General recognized therein the mark of a genius for the warfare of surprise attacks and ambushes. Immediately, he gave his approval: "Degains is right."

"So be it!" said Champeau, still quivering with emotion. "But what are we going to do, exactly?"

"Patience!" murmured Degains, intensely meditative again. "I have an idea; we must let it mature. Go into the garden, will you? Leave me alone. I need to work, estimating certain measurements, by means of guesswork and memory, relative to the plans I've just drawn."

Without paying any more heed to the compliant general, Champeau and Croqui, Jean Degains sat down again at the table, took up the pencil once again and leaned over the white sheet of paper streaked horizontally and vertically by judiciously-assembled black lines.

# Chapter IV: Murder?

When night fell on that Thursday March 21, Leo Saint-Clair was only able to take approximate account of it by the time indicated by the ticking clock on the mantelpiece of the sealed studio, which had been nothing to him but a torture chamber since the morning.

Collapsed in an armchair, feverish, sometimes drowsy but always reawakened with a start by some cruel brutality on the part of the abominable Grigoryi, the unfortunate youth retained all his courage. He was suffering direly from thirst, and hunger was beginning to twist his stomach with dull cramps—which, he knew, would soon become sharper. He was also suffering from the numerous burns that his torturer had inflicted on his arms, his throat, the back of his neck and all over his naked torso, with matches, cigarettes or cigars. In spite of everything, though, his courage was still intact, and his soul was rigid, resolute and invincible.

Besides, a tenacious hope sustained him.

A hundred times during that terrible day he had told himself: *In spite of all the walls, my friends and the police will get in here. Robert, René and Jean can't have forgotten the address that I gave them as I left. The subterfuge mounted by Madame Cheminska will put them off momentarily, but won't obliterate the idea that I put into their heads: that it's at 18, Rue du Fossé, in the Rive neighborhood, that they must look for me. They'll look for me and they'll find me. Until then, I'll be in pain—so be it! Pain is nothing. The real, the great, the only danger is that Grigoryi might have the time to stab me,*

147

*strangle me or blow my brains out when my friends' intervention occurs.*

Then he would meditate, not without a frightful sadness and an invasive anguish: *To die at 20! My dear Mama, my poor Papa! And what regrets I'd have, deep down! That those I love, and who love me, will be so unhappy! The life—the life that I saw before me, so vast, so rich in promises, tasks, exploits...and so beautiful! To die...the future life...eternal life...yes. Well, at least I shall die without talking, and my executioner, his masters and accomplices will have the rage of knowing nothing, of not being able to use my father's invention, the genius of the engineer Pierre Saint-Clair, against France and the civilized world!*

And again, with melancholy irony: *Ah! I haven't been the Nyctalope, the eighth wonder of the world, for very long!*

Then he would start, and would be unable help emitting a cry or a groan, Grigoryi having just applied the incandescent tip of a cigar or a cigarette, or the flame of a match, to his living flesh, while sniggering something along the lines of: "But this is only a foretaste of the torture by fire, my lad! Tomorrow, we'll try the iron bar, red-hot from the blow-torch, and even the moving and penetrating point of the flame projected by the blow-torch. Then, yes, you'll begin to take account of the fact that there might perhaps by six or seven days of those little games. And if you fall unconscious, you know, I'll make sure to revive you, and I'll make you drink a hot and spicy glass of rum, or an infusion of tea, or of mint, and well-sugared and alcoholic condensed milk, in order to build up your strength...so that you can suffer more, and for longer..."

And after a pause, he would conclude, emphasizing his words: "At least until you decide to talk. The secret of Radiant Z, my lad! And then you'll be saved, cared-for and set free! And who will care for you? Who will coddle you? Who will look at you with her big blue eyes full of compassion and intertwine her perfumed fingers with yours? Who? Aurora! The beautiful Aurora Malianova!"

Ah, what an intelligent, perverse and ferocious torturer! And what a tempter!

At the name of Aurora, and the evocation of what Aurora's cares, smiles, gazes and caresses might bring—of the young woman in the immaculate nurse's uniform who had suddenly opened up to him all the perspectives of passion and had caused him to feel the marvelous first stirrings of love—the unfortunate Leo suffered a pain even more violent, profound and tortuous than those of the burns, the thirst and the hunger.

Was he tempted?

Horror! Several times in the course of the long an accursed day he had to struggle, drawing strength from the utmost reaches of his soul, to resist the temptation of letting himself slide down the slope of dangerous dreams and desires…and that was the most difficult and terrible thing of all.

But the hours passed in the progression of that Gehenna. Night finally arrived.

*He'll go to sleep*, Saint-Clair told himself, as he watched his torturer eating and drinking at the table, a little after 8 p.m. *While he sleeps, I'll be tranquil—and perhaps I'll be able to sleep myself, in spite of the hunger, the thirst and the torment of the burns. Dear God, give me that sleep, and then new strength and courage. Dear God, guide my friends to me…*

These reflections, prayers and invocations Leo Saint-Clair repeated until he was distracted from them by Grigoryi.

Having slowly finished eating and drinking, the colossus stood up and came over to his victim.

"You've certainly guessed," he said, "that I shan't be going short of sleep. I need it. It's also necessary for you to sleep, so you'll have enough strength tomorrow. But no tricks! Last night, I gave you the divan and I only slept on an armchair, like a night-watchman on his seat—which is to say, badly. Tonight, old chap, I intend to get the benefit of a good night's sleep, so I'm going to get undressed and go to bed, to surrender myself to the deep and sound sleep to which I'm accustomed. I repeat, though—no tricks. I'll have to tie you up in such a way that you won't be able to get loose and do me a bad turn. Don't move—you'll be perfectly all right in this armchair, you'll see."

He went into the laboratory and came back with cords of various thickness. In a low voice he muttered: "You already have your hands pinned behind you— that's all right. I'll tie your feet together at the ankles, and one of them to the leg of the armchair. Good!" When he had finished, he continued in the same soft tone, as if he were talking to himself: "The shoulders now. The cords will pass over your breast and under your armpits and stick you to the back of the armchair. Perfect, eh? There you are, wedged in for the night. Have pleasant dreams, my boy! Imagine that Aurora, the beautiful, the gentle, the smiling Aurora…"

He said no more.

It would have been better, alas, had it happened later, while he was asleep, but it did not happen not later; it was at that exact moment, as he stood up after having tied the last knots at the back and the foot of the arm-chair, and as he turned toward the laboratory, from which bizarre grating and grinding sounds were coming, that...

A supple shadow bounded out of the laboratory, which was open and illuminated—and a youth with red hair soiled with soot appeared, standing in the full glare, aiming a stout Browning and shouting: "Hands up!"

Then there were 20 seconds of vertiginous and atrocious drama—for Grigoryi had the audacity and the savage temerity not to obey.

As he heard the cry, he raised his head abruptly, with sharp eyes, and threw himself to one side.

The Browning roared, but the bullet shattered the glass of a framed engraving on the wall.

From the table Grigoryi grabbed the knife that he had used during his meal, and another bound brought him face-to-face with Saint-Clair.

The Browning thundered again—and this time, Grigoryi was hit full in the chest. "Damnation!" he swore—and with a violent thrust of his right arm he buried the knife in Saint-Clair's left side.

A third shot resounded. Grigoryi collapsed, with a hole in his forehead.

But Jean Degains, suddenly panic-stricken and desperate, saw both the knife in Leo Saint-Clair's side and the supreme convulsion of his entire body, stiffening within its bonds. Moaning with terror, he looked at the other's face and saw bloodless features, an open mouth, and eyes rolling back...

"My God! My God! Leo! Leo! You aren't dead... Tell me you aren't dead?"

## Conclusion:
## Doctor de Villiers-Pagan's
## Cardiorhythmy

Doctor Cheminska was not arrested, but was interrogated extensively, several times over, by the police and an Investigating Magistrate. She thought she was safe—and she would have been, if Leo Saint-Clair had been dead, for he alone could talk about her, and several other individuals, while knowing what he was talking about.

But Leo Saint-Clair was not dead. And he did not die!

After a minute of panic, Degains had run to a window, opened it, and, seeing the brick wall, presumably made up externally to look like the old wall, he had understood. With heavy blows of a massive oak stool, he had broken through the fake wall and leaned his upper body through the breach, shouting: "Saint-Clair is wounded! Telephone Villiers-Pagan immediately!"

In the courtyard were Champeau, Croqui, the Commissaire of the Special Police and several of his men. Others were keeping Madame Cheminska under surveillance in her own apartment. She had a telephone. It was Champeau who telephoned Doctor de Villiers-Pagan, not in Lausanne but in Geneva, where he had been for two days in order to attend all the sessions and soirées of an international surgical conference.

A quarter of an hour later, the policemen having broken down the false wall at the foot of the staircase—

which Degains had easily discovered—in the meantime Doctor de Villiers-Pagan was beside the still-inanimate Saint-Clair, examining him minutely.

"He's alive!" he said. "Don't touch the knife. The extremity of the blade must be placed between the aorta and the pulmonary vein, which has caused the heart to stop suddenly. Get him to my clinic, quickly."

His large and comfortable limousine was in the street. Without any shock to the knife, Leo Saint-Clair was carried down to and laid out in it, well-secured by numerous cushions. And 70 minutes later, at the clinic, the prodigious operation was carried out. It was the first time that the *resurrection of the heart* had been attempted on a human being.

Doctor de Villiers-Pagan was the inventor and experimenter, in the greatest secrecy, of an apparatus that he called an "artificial heart." He had only tried it out, in order gradually to perfect it, in the breasts of dogs, monkeys and pigs anaesthetized by chloroform—which, on awakening, had lived on, not with their own natural organs, but with hearts of rubber and metal!

Only when he had opened Leo's breast did the surgeon extract the murderous blade, and he fitted to the arteries—in which he had made the necessary incisions—the glass tubes of the artificial and mechanical organ. An electric current and a magnet, immediately activating the alternating movement of the supplementary heart, gradually regulated the afflux and reflux of the still-warm blood within the fortunately-intact heart of the wounded man.

For a long, interminable quarter of an hour, Leo Saint-Clair remained inanimate—but finally, almost imperceptibly at first, then very slowly, the reflexes reappeared and functioned. Although he was under the influence of the chloroform, Leo Saint-Clair presented all the phenomena of sanguinary circulation and respiration— and hence of life!

He had been quite literally brought back to life!

A week later, he was able to talk.

He talked.

Only the nihilist Helena, however, better-known by the title and name of Doctor Olga Cheminska, remained in the hands of the police, because she alone had been kept under surveillance since the tragic night of the twenty-first of March. As for the other spies and nihilists mixed up in the affair of Radiant Z that Saint-Clair was able to identify, they had disappeared. Alexis Roudine's villa was empty. So were Doctor Serge Ivanov's house and the shady café where the subaltern agents of the criminal association met.

The balance-sheet of the affair was as follows:

The documents and apparatus related to Radiant Z were returned to the engineer Pierre Saint-Clair. Alas, though, struck by general paralysis, he was never able to resume his work, and his inventions in that instance were never realized. Leo Saint-Clair knew nothing! It was out of courage, and in order not to turn back the anger and desires of Sadi Khan and his gang on to his father that the sublime fellow had let Grigoryi believe that he was party to the secret!

Sadi Khan was not seen again, nor even identified. Doubtless he must have been, at a later date, among the companions of Lenin during the great revolution that turned Russia upside-down and orientated his destiny toward indiscernible ends.

Wenceslas Polki was never found, his abductors having killed him and thrown his heavily-weighed body into the deepest part of the lake.

As for Mademoiselle Aurora Malianova, when she learned about Jean Degains' cunning via the narrative of the exploit recounted at the clinic, she retired discreetly to her room, in the most natural possible fashion. The next day she was found dead. She had taken a fatal dose of Veronal[11] in an infusion of lime-flowers. It was believed to be a mistake.

And Leo Saint-Clair, who wept for her during long nocturnal hours, never revealed to anyone, save for his historiographer, that the nurse Aurora Malianova was the famous Katia Garcheva, the nihilist. Because she had almost caused his death, and because she had been his first love, he would never forget her, and never found within himself the cruel strength to detest her. For a very long time he must have been convinced that he would never love as profoundly, as sweetly or as desperately as he did in the unique week in which he became the Nyctalope, and in which he experienced passion, death and resurrection.

## THE END

---

[11] Veronal—the best-known of the brand names under which the first barbiturate, discovered in 1903 by Emil Fischer and Joseph von Mering, was marketed—was already notorious in 1912 for causing death by what were conventionally reported as accidental overdoses.

# BLACK AND GOLD

*by Emmanuel Gorlier*

January 15, 1919. 10:25 p.m. The Paris-Barcelona express train rushed through the darkness. The storm above was about to burst; the clouds were speared by sporadic flashes of lightning, while deafening bursts of thunder filled the horizon.

In the berth of a first-class compartment, a man was vainly trying to sleep. His excitement was too great, and he could not keep his eyes from constantly returning to his briefcase. IT was at long last in his possession. IT: the precious document he had finally succeeded in acquiring. It was, of course, encoded, but he had bribed a corrupt officer of the French Deuxième Bureau and now possessed the key to the cipher used by the Black Corsair.

Once again the man reviewed the events of the past few days; in particular, the suspicious behavior of two guests who had suddenly arrived at the hotel where he had been staying and seemed to be spying on him. Some of the staff, too, had seemed much too inquisitive... He had wondered if he was becoming paranoid! Still, he felt he had made the right decision by leaving suddenly without notifying anyone. There was too much at stake! He had left Spain on the first express train to Paris.

Outside, the storm finally burst and heavy drops of water began to fall on the sleeping car in a deluge.

Soothed by the sound of the rain and the rhythm of the train, the Man finally fell asleep.

January 16. 2:15 a.m. Suddenly, the man woke up,. The rain had stopped. The air should have felt lighter, purer, but it was quite the opposite, the man felt sick, his chest burned. He was finding it difficult to breathe. His eyes were tearing. Seized with panic, he rushed to his briefcase, opened it and pulled out a yellowed sheet of paper, covered with figures. The lines seemed blurred. He staggered backward and fell onto his berth. The pains in his chest increased. He thought that if he lie down, he might be able to breathe easier.... But no! Everything grew dark. His hand dropped the precious document for which he had given so much. Seconds later, he was unconscious.

The same day. 9:50 a.m. Two men were sharing a copious continental breakfast in a plush residential house on rue Nansouty in Paris' 14th arrondissement. They both shared a similar, aquiline profile, but one of them had gold-speckled eyes with the acuity of a hawk. His hair was cut short and his face was devoid of facial hair; his companion, however, looked more bohemian and sported a handlebar mustache. The man with the gold-speckled eyes was Leo Saint-Clair, the prodigious explorer known as the Nyctalope because of his uncanny ability to see in complete darkness. His guest was his biographer, the popular novelist Jean de La Hire. They both remained silent, enjoying the warm coffee, the buttered tartines, the croissants and jam that had been laid out for them by Corsat, the Nyctalope's butler. Breakfast was not a time for talking, but for communing with food.

Twenty minutes later, comfortably installed in leather armchairs, they finally began to discuss their business.

"I had a meeting with Férenczi," said La Hire. "He's thrilled at the idea of publishing my novelization of your Martian expedition. I'm still waiting for the contract, but I think the book might come out as early as next year."

"That is good news, Jean," replied Leo gravely. "This publication is important to me; I want the public to learn that the benefits of our French civilization have now been exported to other celestial bodies. I plan to return to Mars someday. There is still much to be done there." Then, after a pause: "Weren't you supposed to introduce me to two of your colleagues?"

"Yes. Captain Cazal and a young writer named Alexandre Zorca; they should be here soon."

Just then, Corsat entered and said:

"Sorry to disturb you, Monsieur, but Monsieur le Président is here and asks to see you at once."

The Nyctalope stood up and offered his hand to Jean de La Hire.

"My dear Jean, I'm sorry to have to cut this meeting short, but pressing matters of state demand my attention. I'll have to meet your friends another time."

La Hire nodded.

"Yes, of course. I know they very much want to make your acquaintance."

"I'll talk to you soon. Good bye!"

As La Hire stepped out of the salon, he politely saluted the Président du Conseil who was rushing in, a grave expression of concern painted on his aristocratic face.

"Monsieur Valenglay, how can I be of service to France?" said the Nyctalope modestly.

"Monsieur Saint-Clair, my car is waiting. You must come with me. It is a matter of the greatest urgency. I will brief you in detail *en route*."

10:30 a.m. A biting, icy wind was blowing through the halls of the Austerlitz Railway station on Paris's left bank. An entire platform had been cordoned off by the police; Leo noticed that the Paris-Barcelona express was stopped there.

At the sight of Monsieur Valenglay and Leo Saint-Clair, the gendarmes saluted and let the two men through.

"Has Doctor Yersin arrived yet?" asked Valenglay.

The Nyctalope was acquainted with Alexandre Yersin, the French physician from the Institut Pasteur who, in 1895, had discovered the bacillus responsible for the dreaded bubonic plague and prepared the first serum. He had met him at his hospital in Hanoi during one of his journeys to the Far East.

"I thought Doctor Yersin as in Indochine?" he remarked.

"Luckily for us he is here on one of his regular visits to the Institut," replied Valenglay.

"He's examining the body," answered the gendarme whom the Président had first addressed. "It's through there."

The Nyctalope and the politician stepped into the sleeping car. They quickly reached the compartment where Doctor Yersin was completing his examination of a dead man.

He turned round when he saw the two men.

"Monsieur Saint-Clair," he said, recognizing the face of the brave, young explorer with pleasure. "What a surprise!"

"Monsieur Saint-Clair has agreed to help us with our investigation," said Valenglay.

"There can be no better choice, Monsieur le Président," replied the scientist. "In Nha Trang, the natives call him *Son Tinh*, the Mountain Spirit."

"Is this a case of Spanish flu, doctor?" inquired Leo.

"No, Monsieur Saint-Clair. It is the most devastating case of pulmonary plague I have ever come across. This poor man was dead in mere hours..." Then, more furtively, he added: "As Monsieur Valenglay will corroborate, there has been a small epidemic in Europe in recent months, which is why the Institut asked me to return to Paris. In order to avoid a panic, we have not told the public and have instead blamed the deaths on Influenza." [12]

"I see," said Leo, then turning towards Valenglay, he asked: "But I'm not a doctor, Monsieur le Président. What can I do?"

Valenglay coughed, took a gum drop from a box in his pocket, then replied:

"Today's case is somewhat different. Monsieur Saint-Clair, and right down your alley, if I may put it that way. You certainly remember a certain Léo de Malterre, a.k.a. The Black Corsair, who, in 1912, stole a prototype submarine of revolutionary design from our Military. That wasn't the first time such a thing happened: the wretched Lupin did the same in 1902, but unlike him, de Malterre declared war upon society because of

---

[12] This did, indeed, occur.

some ill-understood grievances. To further his anarchistic ambitions, he had assembled a vast, criminal organization that trafficked with other, similarly notorious villains from across the globe…"

"I remember that quite well, Monsieur Valenglay. In fact, I, myself, played a modest part in the man's downfall."

"Yes, of course," said the politician. "Then you will recall that eventually, an armistice of sorts was reached with de Malterre and all his men were pardoned. Recently, they have all begun to die, one by one, from this very same strain of pulmonary plague!"

"That is indeed odd."

"But for the first time, we appear to have a clue," said Doctor Yersin. "I found this page, written in some kind of code, amongst the dead man's effects."

In his hand, he held the yellow sheet of paper which the dead man had dropped before succumbing to the fatal disease.

The Nyctalope took the document and studied it with attention. Then, he frowned, as if a thought had struck him. His eyes looked beyond the platform, with its squadron of uniformed men, and focused on the shadow-shrouded rail yard meant for storing, sorting, loading and unloading cars next to the station.

"Do you have any anti-plague serum with you?" he asked the doctor.

"Of course!"

"I'll need an injection," said the Nyctalope, as he pulled up his sleeve.

Later that day. 3:07 p.m. The room was brightly lit by an array of electric lights. Everything in it was made of gold: the table, the chairs, a man-sized safe, presently ajar, revealing its dazzling contents: a collection of gold coins from various eras: doubloons, thalers, *écus*... Even the artworks hanging on the wall were made of painted gold.

In its center was a solid gold statue of a man, struck in a visionary pose, pointing at the horizon as if heralding the dawn of a better day. Next to the statue, sitting in a gold armchair, was a man lost in a reverie, contemplating dark thoughts known only to him; it was in fact the man portrayed in the statue: Doctor Fisturn.

Doctor Fisturn had only one overriding obsession: gold. A promising biologist, he had been recruited by the Black Corsair and worked on the deadly strain of plague for which de Malterre had traded with the enigmatic Asian mastermind known in some parts of the world as "Doctor Natas." During his brief encounters with Natas on behalf of the Black Corsair, Fisturn had learned that the scientist held another secret: he could make gold!

But Natas' secret had been handed over to de Malterre himself on a carefully encrypted sheet of paper!

For seven years, despite the turmoil of the Great War, Fisturn had labored to disentangle the careful network of associates the Black Corsair had gathered around him. One by one, he had hunted these men in the hopes of finally getting his hands on the secret formula that would make him the Gold Maker! The King of the World!

He had used Natas' deadly bacillus to kill all those who refused or thwarted him, or even threatened to expose him. In so doing, innocents had also perished. But as the saying went, it was all about the omelet and not the eggs...

And finally, the formula had been found! The man from Barcelona had it, but he had been disposed of. Men had been sent to fetch it and should be back any minute!

The bell rang.

Fisturn carefully looked through the spy hole: it was his two acolytes, the same men whom the dead agent would have recognized as the two guests who had checked into the hotel in Barcelona late at night. Pressing on a hidden button in his chair, he let them in. Once they were in his sanctum, he asked:

"Do you have it?"

The taller of the two men looked afraid and finally muttered:

"Er, no. The Nyctalope took it."

Fisturn blanched.

"What happened?"

"We followed your instructions to the letter. We checked in at his hotel, bribed the staff and managed to slip the bacillus into his food. But he left suddenly and we missed him at the station. We were forced to take the train after his. By the time we got to the Gare d'Austerlitz, he was already dead and the police had cordoned off the platform, so we hid in the rail yard and kept watch. A doctor arrived, then the Président du Conseil with the Nyctalope. I recognized him at once because I've seen his picture in the newspapers. He took the document and left..."

"Where were you while you were watching all this?" asked Fisturn, suddenly seized by a horrible presentiment.

"Safe in the darkest portion of the rail yard."

"Fools!" shouted the scientist. "Don't you know that..."

"...Darkness does not exist for the Nyctalope!" concluded a strong voice from the other side of the room.

The three men turned round and saw the Nyctalope, smiling, pointing a Browning at them.

"Shoot him!" screamed Fisturn. "He can't get us all before we kill him!"

As the two gangsters grabbed their guns, the Nyctalope shot out the electric array. The room was immediately plunged into total darkness.

"I wouldn't bet on it," said the Nyctalope.

In the dark, the Nyctalope saw Fisturn pull a test tube from his breast pocket.

"I've just been vaccinated by Doctor Yersin," he said. "It won't work."

Fisturn recognized the name of the great French scientist who had vanquished the horrors of the plague and, with a gesture of defeat, placed the test tube on the table.

"We surrender," he said, beaten.

That evening. 7:30 p.m. Leo had just finished dressing for an evening at the Opéra. After straightening his white tie, he grabbed his hat, then the invitation. *I'm impatient to see* Aida *sung by that new diva*, he thought. *She's become the toast of Paris. What's her name already?... Ah yes, Laurence Païli...*

*Translated by Jean-Marc Lofficier*

# MARGUERITE

*By Jean-Marc Lofficier*

January 1942. Vichy had ordered a sweep of the region of Combefontaine, North of Lyon, for members of the Resistance. The Nyctalope was asked to go along; he was not happy because he despised the Milice, but when Jacques de Bernonville had told him that Hugues Mezarek might have returned, he felt he had no choice. He feared that the carnage the fearsome Belzebuth might wreak far exceeded that of Klaus Barbie.

They had been searching the village for an hour when the Nyctalope entered the Loubets' house. The old farmer and his wife looked at him with the hostility he had come to recognize; in a corner, he noticed a small girl playing with a doll.

"What's your name?" he asked the child.

"Laurence," she replied.

"And what's her name?" he said, pointing at the doll.

"Marguerite."

"Can I hold her?"

The child reluctantly gave him the doll. He looked under its skirt. It was made in England.

"Where did you get it?" he said, giving the doll back.

"Yesterday was my twelfth birthday. The Tooth Fairy came in the middle of the night and brought me the doll. He said her name was Marguerite. He kissed me and told me to go back to sleep and not tell anyone."

The Nyctalope stood up. The Milice was about to enter the Loubet house. He looked at the child. He looked at Marguerite.

"Please, Monsieur, take Marguerite for your daughter," said Laurence, shyly handing him the doll. "Maybe she doesn't have a Marguerite."

The Nyctalope took the doll.

"I already searched this house," he told the Milice. "There's no one here except a couple of farmers and their granddaughter. False alarm." Then, he whispered to Laurence: "I'll take Marguerite but only because someone else might wonder what a British doll is doing here. Tell the Tooth Fairy that tonight, the border will be unguarded near Chaumont."

After the War, the Loubets—father and daughter reunited at last—received a package in the mail that contained Marguerite. They searched in vain for the Nyctalope to thank him, but he had vanished.

# THE HEART OF A MAN

*by Roman Leary*

Buenos Aires, 1947. Giraud was enjoying a café chico at *Las Violetas* when the hectoring voice of the Belgian piped up in his mind. *How can you drink that mud, Giraud? You should have a sirop de cassis! There is a drink to delight the senses!*

Giraud cringed and set down his cup. "Why don't you leave me alone?" he muttered to himself. He quickly glanced around when he realized he had spoken aloud, but the other patrons of the elegant coffee house were lost in their own affairs and, to his relief, paid him no heed.

More and more of late, Giraud found himself thinking of the Belgian. It disturbed and annoyed him. He had spent the better part of 20 years trying to forget Hercule Poirot, and now, here, the man was, occupying his mind with all the force and vigor of a memory made only the day before. Worse, he was beginning to carry on active conversations with the little bastard, which was making him worry for his sanity.

*Tut, tut, Giraud*, the Belgian chided. *You should welcome my wise counsel. Perhaps some time in my presence will serve to elevate your modest intellect.*

Giraud ground his teeth. Modest intellect! He had once been called the greatest detective in France, hailed as a modern Vidocq, but then...

*Ah, but then came the Renault case. You were over-confident,* mon ami. *If you had listened to Papa Poirot, you would not have arrested the wrong person. What a famous blunder! How fortunate I was there to save that young man from the guillotine!*

Giraud closed his eyes and began to rub his temples. "That wouldn't have happened," he whispered. "I would have seen the truth in time. I would never send an innocent man to his death. Never..."

"Are you ill, Monsieur Giraud?" a man's voice asked. He was speaking English, unusual in this city...

"I'm quite all right," Giraud snapped. He was embarrassed, and was about to tell the man to leave him alone when he was silenced by a sudden chill.

The man had called him by name.

Giraud had been living in Buenos Aires under an assumed name since 1945. There were only two people in Argentina who knew his true identity, and neither of them owned the voice he had just heard.

Giraud slowly opened his eyes. Standing before him was a tall, powerfully built man in a gray double-breasted suit. He was pale, square-jawed and clean shaven, with a wiry crew-cut that gave him a military air. His black eyes, as round and cold as a shark's, regarded Giraud with analytical detachment. Giraud was a big man, but something in those eyes made him feel small and vulnerable.

*Compose yourself, Giraud,* Poirot said in a soothing, paternal tone. *Let us draw this fellow out, eh? Find out how much he knows.*

Giraud had to admit it was a good strategy. He smiled and chuckled, relaxing into a pose of friendly nonchalance. "I'm afraid you've mistaken me for someone else, sir," he said. "My name is..."

"I have not made a mistake," the man interrupted. He spoke in a slightly reproving tone that, despite its gentleness, hummed with an undercurrent of menace. "You are Henri Giraud, formerly of the Sûreté Nationale. During the German occupation, you worked with SIPO-SD Section Four, the Gestapo in France. When the war was over, you fled here to escape prosecution as a collaborator."

*Our question is answered*, Poirot said. *He knows everything.*

Giraud's heart was hammering. God, what a disaster! Perhaps he could brazen it out. "Of all the impertinence!" he sputtered. "How dare you insult me with these slanderous allegations! And in a public place, at that!" He made an expansive gesture and took the opportunity to glance at the exits. Had those men been there before? It was a warm day, but they were both wearing long coats... He reached into his own jacket and searched for the comforting heft of his only friend, a .25 Beretta. He found nothing but lint.

"Your pistol was removed earlier by one of my associates," the man said, his dark eyes boring into Giraud's skull. "I am sad to say that it was done rather easily."

Giraud felt his front of righteous indignation cracking from the pressure of his rising panic. "I don't have to tolerate this...this..." Words failed him. He started to rise, but the man held up his hand in an unmistakable warning. He then lowered the hand and Giraud, as if hypnotized, followed the motion back into his chair.

"Are you going to continue with these childish theatrics?" the man asked. "Or would you like to stop while you still have some modicum of dignity?"

Giraud opened his mouth to protest, but the words died on his tongue. He sighed heavily, gathered his nerve, and met the stranger's penetrating gaze. "I'm afraid you have the advantage of me, Monsieur...?"

"I have the advantage of most people," the man said. He sat down in the chair opposite Giraud and gestured for a waiter. He ordered water with lemon and stared silently at Giraud while he waited for it to arrive. Giraud began to feel like a naughty schoolboy who had been summoned to the headmaster: *What is this I hear about you working with the Nazis, Henri? And don't tell me everyone else was doing it because that's not an excuse!*

"Do you find something amusing?" the man asked as his water was set before him.

"Merely a random thought," Giraud said. "I would be surprised if you didn't know exactly what it was, since you seem to find me so completely transparent."

"That sounds vaguely like a gibe," the man said with a cold smile, "but it's closer to the truth than you think." He took a sip of his water. "While I may not be able to read your exact thoughts, I certainly know the spirit of them. I have always been able to see into the heart of a man, to know if he is brave or cowardly, honest or a liar."

"Dare I ask what this penetrating insight tells you about me?"

"Your immediate terror at being recognized tells me that you live in the more or less constant fear that you will be caught and punished for your misdeeds. Logically, this fear is absurd. Your contribution to the Nazi machine was fairly inconsequential and hardly merits the sort of aggressive pursuit that would follow you here. You are intelligent enough to know this, but the fear remains. Why?"

Giraud drank some of his coffee. It was beginning to get cold.

"I submit to you that your fear is merely a symptom of your guilt," the man continued. "This is unfortunate. I could use a man like you, but I have no patience for those who indulge in..."

"Stop," Giraud said. "Stop right there. What did you mean by that? That you could use a man like me?"

The man tilted his head slightly. He considered for a moment, then said: "It doesn't matter. I am afraid this interview has been a waste of your time and mine. There is no room in my organization for a man burdened with a conscience." He began to rise from his chair. "Good day, Monsieur Giraud."

"Wait," Giraud said in a firm voice. "If you really know so much, then you must know how I have made a living for the past two years."

"Of course," the man replied. He was standing now, clearly impatient to leave. "You are a private detective."

"Oh, I call myself that," Giraud said with a derisive laugh, "but I'm really just a strong-arm, a hired thug. I earn enough to keep myself fed and clothed, but that's about it."

"What is this supposed to mean to me?"

"What do you think it means? It means I am in need of money, and more than that, a challenge!"

The man looked at his watch. "So?"

Giraud wanted to grab the man's lapels and shake him, but he forced himself to be still, to speak in an even tone. "Well, Monsieur, you have gone to the trouble of seeking me out. I think you should at least let me hear your proposition. If my scruples balk at it, then dismiss me for a fool and leave me to languish in my so-called guilt."

The man looked at Giraud. Was that renewed interest lurking in his eyes, or merely contempt?

*He is looking into your heart,* mon ami, Poirot said softly. *What do you think he sees there?*

The man gave a small nod. "Very well," he said. "Allow me to introduce myself, Monsieur Giraud. My name is Ernst Stavro Blofeld, and I would like to hire you to solve a murder."


In dreams, they love him still...

The party is one of his wife's usual triumphs. Laure can always find the perfect balance between good taste and gross ostentation. The guests practically stand in line to lavish him with praise for the food, the wine, the extraordinary beauty of the hostess... and he cannot stop wishing he were somewhere else.

It has been several months since his confrontation with the power-mad Lucifer; months of newlywed bliss and stupefying boredom. He finds himself secretly hoping for some urgent message, some desperate summons to action that will place him at the center of an epic struggle against a deadly foe. Home and hearth and the marriage bed are all well and good, but for a man such as he, they can never be enough. Perhaps he simply was not made for this sort of domestic...

His thoughts are interrupted by an insistent tapping of silver against crystal. "Your attention, everyone," says a loud, authoritative voice. "Your attention, please." The crowd falls silent as someone steps unsteadily onto a chair. It is his old friend, Prillant. The banker's face is flushed with wine and bonhomie as he addresses the crowd. "I have just learned that our host, Monsieur Leo Saint-Clair, is a proud father-to-be!"

There is an eruption of applause and cheers. Leo waves to the gathering, twisting his grimace into a smile. Why did Laure have to start telling people so soon?

"Hear, hear!" someone in the crowd shouts. "Give us a toast, Prillant! A toast to Leo!"

Prillant grins and raises his glass. "To Leo! A young man who embodies the best of France, and therefore the best of the world! Who can match his heroism, his brilliance, his courage?"

"No one!" they respond, almost in unison.

"Who can boast of a stronger heart?" Prillant asks.

"A heart of steel!" someone shouts back, and Leo unconsciously reaches to his chest. His heart is mostly plastic, actually. But there is steel there as well. It is the only one of its kind, a life-saving gift from a medical genius, a man now long dead. Leo often closes his eyes in the night and concentrates on listening to the electric hum beneath its rhythmic pounding. He sometimes wonders if it will beat forever.

"And who, I ask, can match his extraordinary vision?"

They get the pun and reward it with laughter. His unique ability to see in complete darkness is what has earned him his alias, a name by which he is known around the world.

"To Leo Saint-Clair, better known as the Nyctalope! May he give France many fine sons!"

"To the Nyctalope!" they shout.

He raises a glass in acknowledgement and braces himself for the inevitable flood of congratulations, the endless hand-shaking and back-slapping. His eyes roam over the smiling faces, glowing with admiration, and he sees something that gives him pause.

It is the cool, sardonic gaze of a girl, one of the servers hired for the party. She is young—probably a student, most of them are—and astonishingly beautiful. She gives a small wave. Is that the glint of a wedding ring? No matter. He feels a connection, tenuous but nonetheless immediate and undeniable.

*She understands*, he thinks. He does not know how he knows this, but he is certain it is true. She knows he does not belong here, and she is amused by the irony of it.

Her full, red lips lift in a wry smile. He has just enough time to smile back before the first of the well-wishers come between them.

It takes a full 30 minutes to find his way to her.

And another ten to get her alone.


"It's a mistake to have your men wearing long coats in this weather," Giraud said. "The moment I saw them, I knew they belonged to you."

"Do you feel this knowledge gave you power over me?" Blofeld asked.

Giraud grunted and looked out the window. They were in the backseat of a sleek black Cadillac Sixty Special. It wasn't the most luxurious car that Giraud had ever been in, but it came close. Blofeld's minions—a pair of efficient automatons named Fitz and Carlos—were in the front.

Fitz, the driver, was handsome to point of absurdity. His blonde hair, chiseled jaw, and ice blue eyes were almost a caricature of Hitler's Aryan ideal. Giraud thought it was little wonder the man had survived the war. He had probably spent the entire time modeling for SS recruiting posters.

Carlos was younger and smaller, but Giraud thought he was infinitely more dangerous. Fitz seemed too aloof to think there could be any real danger to himself or his master, but Carlos' eyes were always moving; observing and cataloging everything and everyone around him. His long fingers compulsively clenched and unclenched, as if he were yearning to spot a potential threat so that he could have the pleasure of eliminating it. Giraud had not been surprised to discover that it was Carlos who had lifted his gun.

"You could be the best pickpocket I've ever met," Giraud had said when the little man returned it to him, empty of bullets.

Carlos' only reply was a sneer.

*Tread lightly, Giraud*, Poirot cautioned. *That one can barely contain his eagerness for violence. I would be wary of him if I were you.*

Well, you *are* me, Giraud silently responded. Or at least some noisome part of me, some demon of my sub-conscious...

*Poirot a demon?* Quelle idée!

Oh, for God's sake, will you just shut up!

"Did you say something?" Blofeld asked.

"No," Giraud said, with perhaps a little too much vehemence. "Tell me, where are we going?"

"Villa Soldati, one of the southwestern barrios."

"I know where it is."

"The murder was committed there, in a small apartment on Escalada Street. The victim was one of my employees, a fellow named Edouard Boucher."

"A Frenchman?"

"Yes," Blofeld affirmed, "a former collaborator, like yourself."

Giraud snorted. "Fond of that word, aren't you?"

"Does the term bother you?"

"I've been called worse."

"That doesn't answer my question."

Giraud sensed he was being tested. What the Hell did the man want him to say? "All right then, it infuriates me," he said defiantly. "I had a job to do and I did it. Crime in Paris didn't just disappear when the Nazis marched in, you know. Someone still had to investigate the robberies, the rapes, the murders."

"So your wartime activities were limited to routine police work?"

Giraud hesitated. "For the most part," he said.

Blofeld turned to him. "And the parts that weren't?"

Giraud turned back to the window.

"Fitz," Blofeld said, "stop the car at the next intersection."

"I helped them find Jews," Giraud said.

"I beg your pardon?"

Giraud turned and looked at Blofeld. "I helped the Gestapo hunt down and arrest Jews. At first, it was only a few, then more and more. Finally, it was entire families. Is that what you wanted to hear?"

"I wanted the truth. I require complete honesty from all of my subordinates."

"Well, now you have it. Do you still intend to eject me at the next intersection?"

"Eject...?" Blofeld's eyes narrowed. "No," he said. "I am curious to hear your opinion on this case. If you can give a suitable demonstration of your skills, I may take you further into my confidence."

"And if I disappoint you?"

"Then I will terminate our association."

*Me, I do not like the sound of that*, Poirot whispered.

Nor do I, Giraud replied.

He turned back to the window and watched the passing buildings, the bustling throngs on the sidewalks. The setting Sun cast a pulsing red radiance over it all.

The rising Sun shines through the curtains of Leo's small apartment on the rue Vavin. It warms his face as he lies on the bed, resting in a state of pleasant languor from his exertions the night before. A shadow passes over his eyes and he turns to see Nina, her exquisite form rendered in silhouette before the window.

"There are some men on the street," she says. "I think they might be Gestapo."

"So? They're everywhere in Paris these days. Come back to bed."

"What if they're looking for you?"

"Impossible. They don't know about this place, and even if they did, it wouldn't matter. They would only want me for some trivial assignment. I could put them off."

She turns to look at him, slightly amazed. "How can you be so cavalier? You speak of them as if they were harmless children, but if they ever decided you were no longer useful to them…"

He smiles at her. "They don't have the power to decide my fate."

The amazement fades into skepticism. For a moment she looks just as she did at the party, all those years ago…

She had been cheerfully cynical even then, and surprisingly unimpressed by his heroic reputation. This, of course, had only made her all the more alluring and soon he was applying the full force of his personality to seducing her. The conquest was inevitable, but no less satisfying for it. What followed was something of a surprise: He was never able to completely let her go.

In the intervening years, he had been through many wives and lovers, but she had proven to be a constant. When he wanted someone with whom he could share his moments of greatest triumph—or rare moments of failure—she always seemed to be the one he reached for. Even more than her sexual prowess, which was considerable, he was drawn to her by her fierce intelligence, and by a sense that there were passages of her soul that he could never travel, never claim.

He might even have married her, if he could have ever persuaded her to leave her lout of a husband. He was always baffled, and slightly piqued, by her stubborn refusal to divorce the man. That she felt guilt over her infidelity was perhaps understandable, but why should she punish herself by staying in a tedious union with an absolute clod? He has asked her this very question, many times, and the answer is always the same:

*Because I love him, you fool. If you had ever really loved anyone yourself you would understand.*

But I love you, he would sometimes protest.

*Ha! You love pleasure, and excitement, and obedience. I give you these things, so you think you love me.*

This last always came with a smile that lessened its sting, and was almost always followed by a touch that rendered further conversation impossible.

She is not smiling now, however. "Why do you do it?" she asks. "Why do you work with them? Do you really believe in them, in their ideals?"

"Does your husband?" He regrets the words as soon as they leave his mouth. It is a cheap evasion, and unworthy of him. He expects her to erupt with fury, but she merely sighs and sits on the bed.

"I tried to talk him out of it, you know. 'The *Milice* are nothing but lackeys for the *boche*,' I said to him. 'If you join those brutes, you will have sold your soul to the Devil.' But it was useless. 'You always think you're smarter than me,' he said. 'Even when we were children, you always thought you were smarter than me...' "

She trails off into silence, staring into some invisible distance. Then she slowly turns to him. "He is right," she says. "I have always patronized him, condescended to him. He says I treat him more like a mother than a wife. Perhaps if I had shown him more respect he would not feel that he had to..."

"Oh, he is an idiot!" Leo says, impatient with this nonsense. "He should listen to your advice. The *Milice* are the most hated *collabos* in the country. When the war is over, they'll be lucky if every one of them doesn't go to the guillotine."

"And what about you?" she asks, her voice rising. "What about the great and mighty Nyctalope? You've never really believed the Nazis could win, so why do you serve them?"

"I am a free agent! I don't *serve*..."

"Yes, you do!" she shouts. "You dare to judge my husband? You are the biggest *collabo* of them all!"

"You think I could do more good by running around in the woods with the Resistance? Don't be naïve. I despise this regime, but by working within it, I have saved hundreds of French lives!"

"Yes, and allowed yourself to become a propaganda tool for people who have slaughtered millions!"

He gawks at her stupidly. She has never spoken to him this way. No one has, in fact.

"You make me sick!" she cries, tears flowing freely down her cheeks. "You boast of your battles against men like Lucifer and Belzebuth, but what are they next to Hitler? Nothing! But do you raise a hand against the Nazis or their Vichy puppets? Oh, no. You might have to give up your fine house, and your fine car, and your..."

He slaps her. Not very hard, but hard enough. There is a moment of arctic silence, then, refusing to meet his eyes, choking with sobs, she quickly throws on her clothes. At the door, she turns to face him. "I used to worship you," she says in a quavering voice, the voice of a wounded child. "I pretended not to, but I did. I knew what we were doing was wrong, but I could never resist you, never turn you away..." She shakes her head. "I thought you were a hero."

He rises from the bed, reaching for her, but she turns her back and walks away.

He stares after her for a moment, listening to her footsteps recede down the hall. Is this the last he will ever see of her? Most likely, he decides, and the thought fills him with a sudden and profound sadness. He tells himself that this is absurd. He can easily find a replacement for her, a younger, more attractive...

He shakes his head. *Do not lie to yourself*, he thinks. *She was the only one left from the old days, the only one who hadn't fallen away. And now she's gone.*

He goes to the door and closes it. When he turns, he notices something on the nightstand, a glint of sunlight on metal. What is that? A necklace?

It is a locket. He opens it and sees two exquisite cameos; one depicting Nina, the other an image of her husband.

He smiles slightly. This is something she will want back. It will provide a face-saving pretext for her to call him, and when she does, he will do whatever it takes to make amends. They will apologize to one another, enjoy a passionate reconciliation, and things will be as they were before.

He is certain of it.

Fitz opened the door to the apartment and was unable to stop himself from gagging. The death stench that hung in the warm, stagnant air was thick, repulsive, almost tangible.

Giraud had known what to expect, and was able to maintain a mask of indifference. He noted with satisfaction that Carlos was looking green. Blofeld, however, remained a model of iron self control. *Smell something?* he might have said. *Why yes, now that you mention it. Is there a corpse around here, by any chance?*

There was. It was lying face down in the small living area, surrounded by Spartan furnishings overturned in almost artful disarray. The lean, sinewy frame was loosely clad in a cheap bathrobe, sodden and sticky with drying blood. Giraud stepped closer and his eyes widened. The man's hair had been cut away from his head, and none too gently. There were large, gory patches where the flesh had been hacked from the skull.

"Has anything been touched?" Giraud asked.

"Nothing," Blofeld replied. "Carlos discovered the body at approximately 8 a.m. He reported it to me immediately."

"Are you certain Carlos didn't kill him?"

The little man glared at Giraud, murder blazing in his eyes.

"I am positive he did not," Blofeld said blandly.

Giraud gave Carlos a benign smile. "Nothing personal, my friend. One has to explore every possibility, no?" He turned to Blofeld. "Has anyone spoken to the neighbors? I'm surprised they haven't called the authorities."

"The other tenants have been persuaded that *we* are the authorities," Blofeld assured him. "They were very cooperative with our initial inquiries. We have learned that there was a brief disturbance around midnight—some shouting, perhaps a cry of pain. The noises ended almost as quickly as they began and so no one took very much note of them."

Giraud had other questions, but he decided to delay them until after a thorough inspection of the scene. He gently turned over Boucher's corpse.

*Beaten beyond recognition*, Poirot observed. *The work of a hammer, perhaps?*

Could be, Giraud replied. Bruising around the neck indicates strangulation. What is that between his front teeth? Gold? Damned odd place for a filling. Oh well...

*The left wrist is broken.*

Yes, and the right arm is severely dislocated. His fist is clenched. I wonder if...

Giraud took out a penknife and worked at the fingers. It was a gruesome task, nearly impossible due to the rigor, but he managed to open the hand. Clutched in the palm, held so tightly that it cut into the flesh, was a locket on a broken chain. He opened it and held it up to the light.

*Shell cameos*, Poirot said. *Is the man our victim?*

I think so.

*The woman, she is quite the beauty.*

She must be a wife or sweetheart that he left behind. He must have been thinking of her as he died. Tragic, but no help to us.

*Is that what you think?*

I fail to see what else we can make of it. Here, let's examine the rest of the scene...

Giraud spent the next the next two hours exploring the apartment with exacting thoroughness. He picked, he crawled, he sniffed. He asked questions about Boucher's habits, his vices, his enemies. Blofeld gave polite, detailed, and uniformly unhelpful answers to all his queries. Boucher was dull and bellicose, but he had no real enemies. He drank, but not to excess. He liked women, but only prostitutes. He was a competent and reliable henchman who knew his role and performed it well.

"Did you consider him a friend?" Giraud asked as, lying prone, he inspected the fibers of a cheap rug.

Blofeld seemed genuinely nonplused. "Friend?" he said, as if he had never heard the word before.

Giraud rose to his knees. "Yes," he said. "Did you like the man? It's not such an odd question, is it?"

"He was an employee. I neither liked nor disliked him."

"Then why are you so concerned with finding his killer? Why not simply let the police handle it?"

"I see," Blofeld said with a nod. "Monsieur Boucher was a strong and capable fighter. Yet, in spite of this, someone came here last night and crushed him like an insect. I would like to meet that someone."

"For revenge?"

Carlos laughed. Blofeld silenced him with a glance. He turned back to Giraud and said: "Do not concern yourself with my motives. I would like to discuss your conclusions. Have you drawn any?"

185

Giraud stood up and brushed off his pants. "I do not believe this crime will ever be solved," he said.

"Why is that?" Blofeld asked, clearly displeased.

"According to you, this man had no friends, no enemies, and—outside of yourself—almost no acquaintances. There was nothing remarkable about his vices, his virtues, or even his personality. He was, in short, a dependable plodder."

"True enough, but I'm not sure I see your point."

"This man is a non-entity. Why would anyone want to mutilate him so?" Giraud pointed at the body. "What is the motive for this crime? Theft? Impossible. What little there is of value has not been touched. Passion? Excited by what, I may ask? Was someone jealous because he slept with their favorite whore?" Giraud made a face to show his opinion of the theory. "This leaves us with revenge."

*Yes, it certainly does,* Poirot interjected.

"Revenge for what?" Giraud continued. "The only person we can ask is lying there, and even if he could speak, I doubt he would give a satisfactory answer." Giraud shook his head. "No, my friends, this was the work of a random lunatic, a madman who, in all probability, will only be caught after he has killed many more in a similar manner."

*A brilliant deduction, Giraud! You have outdone yourself!*

"It is the only explanation. What else can account for this butchery? I have never seen anything…"

*Go on, Giraud. This is most edifying.*

Giraud was silent. He stared at Boucher, at the shorn, bloody scalp.

*You were about to say you had never seen anything like it before, no?*

Giraud walked over to the corpse, knelt beside it, and looked once more into the broken ruin of the mouth. He took out his penknife and worked at the shattered teeth, removing a small piece of gold. He held it close to his eyes, studied it for a long moment, then closed his hand around it with a sigh.

"Is there something you would like to tell me?" Blofeld asked with an edge of impatience.

"I was wrong," Giraud said.

"About what?"

"Everything."

*Bravo! Now you are using your little gray cells!*

The morgue attendant is an old man, but surprisingly wiry and athletic. His iron-gray eyes, the same shade as his thinning hair, look up from a clipboard at the sound of Leo's approach. They regard him first with curiosity, then suspicion.

"I know you," he says. "Your name is…"

Leo waves it away. "Please," he says. "I received a call. There is someone here. My address was in her things. My number."

The old man frowns. "Name?" he says, all business now.

Leo tells him, and the old man gives him a curt nod. He turns and gestures for Leo to follow. They walk between the rows of shrouded corpses. *So many*, Leo thinks. *Does this many die in Paris every day?*

They pass a pair of nuns praying over one of the bodies. Their breath condenses in the cold, their words turning to wisps of white vapor. Was the dead man a priest? Leo wonders. Did he live long enough to celebrate the defeat of the Nazis, to offer up a prayer of thanks for the Liberation?

One of the nuns, a frail young slip of a girl, glances up and notices Leo. He sees in her haunted eyes a light of recognition, which quickly darkens into smoldering ashes. There is an accusation in that gaze that confuses and angers him. He quickly looks away.

The attendant stops so abruptly that Leo almost bumps into him. "Here," the man says, pointing at a body wrapped in white.

"I want to see her," Leo says.

"I don't recommend it."

"I don't give a damn what you recommend."

"Suit yourself. Do you want the shroud removed or simply pulled back?"

"Remove it."

The man obeys and Leo feels the blood drain from his face.

Her head has been shaved. Her face—her sweet, beautiful face—is mottled and bruised. Swastikas have been tattooed on her breasts and stomach. Leo turns away, sickened by the obscenity of it.

"I warned you," the old man says, pulling up the shroud.

"So you did," Leo says, suppressing the urge to break the man's jaw. "Do you know anything about it, about this..." he gestures at the body.

"The *tonte*—the head-shaving—it's been happening a lot, you know. Now that the allies have driven out the *boche*, people want their revenge. Any woman suspected of being a *collabo* is in danger of losing her hair... and sometimes more."

"She wasn't a collaborator," Leo says.

"She was married to a *Milicien*," the man replies in a matter-of-fact tone. He is not looking at Leo. He is completely focused on re-wrapping the body. "There was a group of men. They broke into his apartment looking for him. She stalled them while he fled. They would surely have killed him if it wasn't for her."

Leo sees it play out like a film before his mind's eye. He watches the coward leaping out a window, leaving her there to defend him against the killers. He sees Nina staring at the door, watching it crack and buckle from the pounding of the vengeful mob. He imagines himself there, as if by doing so he could somehow change the outcome.

*Run!* he cries. *You still have time! Go to our place on the rue Vavin! You still have a key! They will never...*

*No,* she says sadly. *I cannot. If I don't slow them down, they will catch him.*

*To Hell with him! Why should you sacrifice yourself for him?!*

She gives him a wan smile. *Because I love him, you fool. If you had ever really loved anyone yourself, you would understand.*

The door collapses and they tumble clumsily into the room, shouting and snarling. They pass through him like the phantom he is, and set about their brutal work.

He is snapped out of his grim reverie by the voice of the attendant. "I'm sure they didn't intend to kill her," the old man says. He is smoothing out the white cloth, folding, tucking. "The *tonte* is more about humiliation than violence. She must have provoked them somehow. Perhaps she goaded them in order to give her husband more time to run away."

"You make it sound as if she brought this upon herself," Leo says. There is a warning in his voice, but the man doesn't seem to hear it.

"Perhaps she did," he says.

"Old man," Leo says, "you are very close to ending the day on one of these slabs."

The man does not look up from his work. "A fierce threat," he says quietly. "Was she one of your lovers? They say you have had many."

Leo is amazed at the man's gall. "What was it you said a moment ago, about goading and provocation?"

The man pauses to inspect the shroud. "You are right to be angry," he says. "I am being rude and insensitive. It is unforgivable that I should speak this way to a national hero." He chuckles softly. "You know, my son was a great admirer of yours. When he was a little boy, he used to say, 'Papa, when I grow up I will be just like the Nyctalope!' He thought you were the best man in France, even after you gave your allegiance to Vichy."

The attendant slowly lifts his head, and looks directly into Leo's eyes.

"My son," he says quietly, "was married to a Jew. At first, I didn't approve, but over time I learned to accept her, even to love her. They had two children, beautiful little girls. Would you like to know what happened to them, my son and his family?"

Leo says nothing.

"This woman had a better death than they did," the old man says. "I do not feel sorry for her. If you wish to kill me for it, then do so. If not, then leave. You have seen what you came here to see."

Leo turns on his heel and walks away into an all-consuming darkness.

Giraud stood at the door facing into the apartment. "The door was not forced," he said. "The killer was able to talk Boucher into opening it for him."

"We had surmised as much," Blofeld said.

Giraud ignored him. The scene was taking shape in his mind, almost as if he witnessed it himself. "They spoke for a moment, then the killer held this up to Boucher, held it before his eyes." Giraud lifted the locket. "Boucher grabbed it with his right hand. The links snapped, but part of the chain remained entwined in the fingers of the killer."

"What happened then?" Fitz asked, caught up in the moment. It was the first time Giraud had heard the man speak. He looked at the German with surprise, then almost laughed when he saw that Carlos and Blofeld were doing the same.

*Well, do not leave him in suspense, Giraud,* Poirot said.

Giraud nodded. "The killer caught Boucher's hand and gave his arm a violent twist." Giraud pantomimed the action, stepping into the role of the murderer. "Boucher's arm was dislocated. The pain was excruciating, but he tried to counter with vicious blow from his left. The killer, however, was too fast for him. He caught Boucher's fist and snapped his wrist with contemptuous ease."

Giraud could almost feel the bones crack beneath his fingers as he mimicked the deed. The sensation was uncanny, godlike. Was this how the Belgian felt when the pieces began to fall into place, when everything sharpened into almost painful clarity? If so, then he could almost forgive the man his arrogance.

"Boucher cried out in pain," he continued, "but only once. After that, things happened so quickly he barely had a moment to breathe. The killer grabbed him by the neck and sent a series of sledgehammer blows into his face. The pounding was so brutal that it actually drove a link from the chain—the chain still clinging to the killer's hand—between what was left of Boucher's front teeth. It remained lodged there until I pried it free a moment ago."

Blofeld picked at some lint on one of his lapels. "And then?" he asked, stifling a yawn.

Giraud stood over Boucher's corpse. "By now, the killer was in the grip of an uncontrollable, psychotic fury. He allowed Boucher to fall, then straddled him, pulled out a knife and..." He pointed at Boucher's head.

"Do you think the killer was a Red Indian?" Fitz asked. He was clearly impressed by Giraud's performance.

"What the Hell do you know about Indians?" Carlos asked.

"I read about them in Karl May," Fitz said defensively. "And I'll thank you not to take that tone. You have no right to..."

"Silence," Blofeld said. His voice was calm and even, but his men obeyed him as if he were Zeus bellowing from Olympus.

"The killer was a Frenchman," Giraud said.

Blofeld's eyes widened. Only a little, but they widened. "How do you know that?"

"Boucher's head was shaved in imitation of *la tonte*, a punishment meted out to women who had collaborated with Nazis during the occupation."

"That seems a bit illogical. Why would anyone do that to Boucher?"

"Because of this," Giraud said, and he held up the locket. "I thought this belonged to Boucher, but it was brought here by the killer. It was in his possession. I think the killer had an attachment to the woman represented in this cameo. I believe this woman was punished for her association with Boucher, and the killer was infuriated by it. He wanted Boucher to suffer the same way she did."

Blofeld stared at Giraud for a long, silent moment.

*I don't think he is convinced,* Poirot said. *Your theory is too weak. It covers all the facts, but it is ultimately just a series of melodramatic suppositions. Where is your evidence?*

"Well, are you going to answer me?" Blofeld asked.

"What?" Giraud said, blinking. "I'm sorry, could you repeat the question?"

"I said, where is your evidence?"

"I expect it to walk through that door later tonight."

Blofeld no longer looked bored or irritated. "Why do you say that?"

"I am employing an old theory," Giraud said with a thin smile, "the one which states that the killer always returns to the scene of the crime." He held up the locket. "Especially when there is something there that he wants back."

They keep him around for a while, pretending that things are the same. He is simply too useful to discard. They tell him his future is secure. *Just stay out of the public eye,* they say. *Time will pass and the people will forgive you.*

*But I don't need forgiveness,* he says. *I haven't done anything wrong.* The words hang flaccid in the air, sounding lame even to his own ears.

They only stare at him. A couple of them sigh and shake their heads, as if he were senile or insane. *Please, don't argue. Just do as we ask. Do that and everything will be all right.*

They are wrong. It is not all right. People have long memories and deep resentments, and one evening, some gray and faceless men in gray and colorless suits come calling.

*In 48 hours you will be arrested*, one of them says. *There is to be a trial, very public and very humiliating. If you would like to avoid this, leave immediately.*

*Very well*, he says. *If I am needed, I can be reached by my Loire Valley contact...*

The gray man holds up his hand. *We don't mean leave Paris*, he says. *Leave France. And never return.*

They walk away before he can recover himself enough to form a reply. Later, he will not even remember packing his bags, checking his guns, or setting the house on fire before driving away.

He travels far and goes through many identities and a great deal of money, and one night he finds himself in a dive bar in Buenos Aires, watching a man across the room chat up an attractive whore.

There is something very familiar about this man, something with unpleasant associations…

The man looks in his direction.

*You.*

The man looks back at the whore. Laughing. Drinking. Enjoying life.

*I remember you.*

The whore whispers something in the man's ear and he shakes his head, pulling out his pockets to show how little they contain. She shakes her head in disgust and turns away.

*You son of a bitch.*

The man shouts something after her, grumbles some unintelligible curses, then heads for the door.

Finishing his drink, Leo Saint-Clair, the Nyctalope, rises and follows him into the night.

Giraud stared at the door until his eyes were dry. He no longer smelled the death stench, although it certainly had not dissipated. All he could think about was Boucher's killer, and how badly he wanted the man to appear.

*The watched pot, it never boils*, Poirot said.

Maybe, Giraud acknowledged, but I don't care. I don't care about anything but seeing that door open.

*And if it does, what then, my friend?*

Then I will have been right, by God! And whatever happens after that is Blofeld's problem.

Blofeld did not seem to be in any suspense at all. He was, to all appearances, perfectly content to sit in the darkness facing the door, calmly waiting to see if Giraud's theory would bear fruit. Giraud did not know how long the man was prepared to wait, and he did not dare to ask. He and the others had not been invited to sit, and so they stood like sentries; Fitz beside the door, Giraud and Carlos flanking Blofeld. Blofeld's henchmen were both armed with automatics, but they had not seen fit to return Giraud's bullets. Under ordinary circumstances, Giraud would have felt naked and helpless, but now nothing mattered except the door.

The door...

The door to the apartment silently opened. A tall shadow stepped inside, and paused at the threshold. Giraud felt a trickle of sweat run down the side of his face. He and the others were concealed in the darkness, but the shadow acted as if it could see them.

Blofeld must have sensed it as well, for he chose that moment to speak. "Please come in," he said. "We are not your enemies."

"Then why are you pointing guns at me?" the shadow replied. "That doesn't seem very friendly."

"I think it's a sensible precaution, under the circumstances. May we talk?"

The shadow confidently walked into the room, picked up one of the overturned chairs, and sat down in front of Blofeld.

"Fitz," Blofeld said, "please close the door and turn on a light."

Fitz obeyed and Giraud was unable to prevent himself from gasping in astonishment. The man sitting before him was older than he remembered. His face was lined and careworn, and there was more than a hint of gray in the swept-back hair. The Mephistophelean goatee was a recent addition, and it leant his classical features a slightly sinister cast. The leather jacket draped over his muscular frame was, like his faded jeans, a far cry from the expensive, tailored clothes he used to be seen in. But, for all that, he was still instantly recognizable. He had once been among the most famous men in France.

"So," Blofeld said, "Monsieur Leo Saint-Clair. It is a pleasure to meet you."

"The pleasure is all yours," the Nyctalope replied. He crossed his arms and legs. He seemed completely at ease. "I see I was expected."

"We were expecting someone, not you specifically." Blofeld gestured to Giraud, who stood at his right. "The credit must go to Monsieur Giraud. He maintained that you would come here tonight."

Saint-Clair turned his eyes on Giraud. "You used to be with the Sûreté," he said.

Giraud was shocked. "You know me?"

"Only by reputation." He turned back to Blofeld. "Who are you?"

"Does the code name *Rahir* mean anything to you?"

Saint-Clair nodded. "An espionage network that operated during the war. What of it?"

"It was my creation."

"Good for you. It was very efficient, while it lasted."

"And very profitable. But my work didn't end with *Rahir*. In fact, I am currently putting together a group–a special executive, if you like–which will direct an enterprise far greater in scope and impact than any network that has ever existed."

"What does this have to do with me?"

"I would like for you to be a part of it."

Saint-Clair's mouth turned in a half-smile of amusement. "I'm not a spy," he said.

"I didn't come here looking for a spy," Blofeld said. He pointed at Boucher. "I came to find the man who did this. I wanted to meet a skilled and ruthless killer whom I could recruit for my organization; a man with an aptitude for terrorism…revenge…extortion…"

The Nyctalope's smile faded. "And you think I am that man?"

"I know that you have the instincts of a mercenary," Blofeld replied. "Anyone who has followed your career can see that."

"Is that so?"

"Oh, I am aware that you were once a well-known champion of the law," Blofeld said with a dismissive wave. "I'm sure that role that was both useful and expedient. I've played it myself, once or twice. However, I think the work you've done on Boucher is ample evidence that you're ready to dispense with that particular artifice. Why don't we move to some more congenial surroundings where we can discuss…"

"This has to be a mistake," Giraud said, shaking his head.

Blofeld looked up at him, his pale face growing red with anger. "Do not open your mouth again while I am speaking," he said. His voice was level, but only just.

"But this can't be right," Giraud said, unfazed. "This isn't... This man is no murderer! He couldn't possibly have done this!" He turned an appealing gaze on the Nyctalope. "Tell him," he said. "You're conducting your own investigation, aren't you? You're hunting a mad killer, and the trail led you here. This is the first time you've even been to this apartment, right?"

Saint-Clair's mouth opened as if he were about to speak, but nothing came out.

"Carlos," Blofeld said, "please silence this jabbering fool."

Carlos smiled and turned his pistol on Giraud. Saint-Clair leapt from his chair, but the little man moved like a cobra. He snapped the pistol around and fired a single shot into the heart of the Nyctalope. Saint-Clair dropped like a stone.

For a moment, they all stood frozen in tableau. Blofeld sighed and pinched the bridge of his nose. "Well," he said, "that was regrettable."

"I'm sorry, sir," Carlos said. "It was instinct. When I saw him move I..."

"There is no need for an apology," Blofeld said, rising to his feet. "I have serious doubts that he could have been turned to my purpose anyway. I could tell that he was still clinging to the shreds of his personal myth. I could see it in his heart." He turned to Giraud with a sneer. "As for you..."

He was interrupted by a stirring on the floor. He looked at Carlos. "Impossible," the little man said, stepping over to the Nyctalope. He leaned over the body. "That shot should have..."

He never finished his sentence. In the span of a heartbeat, Saint-Clair's hands had closed around Carlos' pistol, driving it up and back into the little man's mouth. There was a thunderclap of gunfire and the back of Carlos' head exploded.

Blofeld, with a speed that belied his hulking frame, grabbed Giraud and shoved him toward the Nyctalope, who was struggling to cast aside Carlos's body. Giraud fell over Saint-Clair, giving Blofeld a few precious seconds to get to the door. "Kill them!" he shouted to Fitz as he ran by.

Fitz fired and Giraud felt a blaze of white heat as the bullet took off the top of his right ear. He fully expected the next one to catch him between the eyes. He was raising his hands before his face in a futile gesture of defense, when he saw a small crimson hole appear on the German's forehead, and a spray of blood coat the wall behind him. Fitz, his face still set in the concentration of aiming, collapsed in a lifeless heap.

The Nyctalope rose slowly to his feet and looked down at Giraud. He pulled a handkerchief from his pocket and wiped his face, which was drenched in Carlos' blood. "It's good that you were in his line of fire," he said to Giraud, dabbing at his eyes. "That probably saved us both."

Giraud fought the urge to start laughing. He had never been so close to death, and his narrow escape had left him in a euphoric state that was close to hysteria. He jumped to his feet and grabbed the Nyctalope's hand, pumping it vigorously. "My God!" he said, grinning. "My God, but that was incredible! How did you survive that shot from Carlos? Are you wearing a bulletproof..."

Giraud fell silent as he noticed the dark, spreading stain on Saint-Clair's chest.

"I will not die from that wound," the Nyctalope said. "My heart is mostly made of plastic. But there is steel there as well."

Giraud was awestruck. "We must get you to a doctor," he said. "Come, let us-"

"No," Saint-Clair said firmly. "I can take care of myself. But before I go, there is something here that belongs to me. Do you have it?"

Giraud began to feel lightheaded. "Something...? No, no, I don't know what you're talking about. Come on, you don't know what you're saying. We need to get you to a hosp..."

The Nyctalope's hand was suddenly at his throat. "That man said you knew I would be here tonight," he whispered. "If that's true, then you must know what I came for. Where is it?"

Giraud reached into his pocket and produced the locket. Saint-Clair released him and took it. He gazed at it for a moment, then dropped it into his coat. He turned and walked toward the door.

"You *did* do it," Giraud said, his voice shaking. "I didn't want to believe it, didn't want to think that you could...You beat that man to a pulp, mutilated him, and left him for dead. What kind of a man are you?"

The Nyctalope stopped. "What kind of man are *you*?" he asked without turning around. "A washed up old *collabo* working as a lackey for a terrorist. Who are you to judge me?"

Giraud's eyes were stinging, and his wounded ear felt as if it were on fire. "I'm nobody," he said. "A washed up old *collabo*, just as you say. But I thought you were better than me. I thought you were a hero."

Saint-Clair turned and looked into Giraud's eyes. His features softened for a moment, and Giraud saw him as he once was; a handsome young Charlemagne, immortal, invincible.

"I thought that too," the Nyctalope said with a sad smile. "I suppose we were both wrong."

A moment later, Giraud was alone with the dead men.

What do I do now? he wondered.

*I will tell you, Giraud,* Poirot said. *You thank the good God that you are alive, and you leave this place before you find yourself answering some very awkward questions.*

Giraud took his advice.

Removing the bullet is difficult and painful, but he manages. *I have survived far worse,* he tells himself, but that does not lessen the agony of each breath.

He lies on the bed in his small basement apartment, blood and sweat soaking through the bandages. There are no lights in that cool darkness, but he can see as clearly as if it were midday, so he keeps his eyes shut tight. Helped along by a generous amount of inexpensive liquor, he topples into a restless, fitful sleep.

The pain follows him into his slumber, and yet, in spite of this, there are times in the night when he smiles.

For in his sleep, he dreams.

And in dreams, they love him still.

# Afterword

## Further Considerations on the
## Life and Times of the Nyctalope

*L'Assassinat du Nyctalope* [*The Assassination of the Nyctalope*], translated here as *Enter the Nyctalope*, was Jean de La Hire's eleventh novel to feature his signature hero, Leo Saint-Clair, a.k.a. The Nyctalope.

The Nyctalope had made his first appearance in *Le Mystère des XV* (translated as *The Nyctalope on Mars*, ISBN 978-1-934543-46-7) (1911). La Hire initially intended the book to be a straightforward science fiction story taking place in the "future," i.e.: the 1930s, but, perhaps bowing to editorial pressure, he changed his mind in mid-stream and firmly relocated the narrative in the present.

That had the effect of pushing back in time by 25 years the previous novel in the saga, *L'Homme qui peut vivre dans l'eau* [*The Man Who Could Live Underwater*] (1909), which had featured the Nyctalope's father, Jean Saint(e)-Clair(e). Thus, in one stroke of the pen, Leo's fictional birthdate had become 1877, instead of the late 1890s.

In the Black Coat Press edition of *The Nyctalope vs. Lucifer* (ISBN 978-1-932983-98-2), we offered a biography and timeline of the Nyctalope's adventures, while noting that there were other works by Jean de La

Hire, whose connections to Leo's life remained to be investigated.

Thanks to the research of French scholar Emmanuel Gorlier, we are now able to add several more books to the list. First of these is *Le Corsaire Sous-Marin* [The Underwater Corsair], serialized by Ferenczi in 1912-13, then again in 1936-37.

In 1912, Léo de Malterre, a.k.a. The Black Corsair, steals a prototype submarine of revolutionary design from the French Navy, then declares war upon society. To further his anarchistic designs, de Malterre assembles a vast, criminal organization. Eventually, an armistice of sorts is reached with de Malterre and all his men are pardoned. The short story *Black and Gold* by Gorlier in this volume references these events.

Leo makes an appearance in issue No. 36 of the serial, when he comes to reclaim the body of his friend, Roger Ciserat. He also finds the so-called "scientific testament" of the great scientist Korridès, which Ciserat had somehow obtained. Leo then goes on to give Korridès' scientific secrets to the French Government.

After World War I, the Nyctalope returned in the aforementioned *The Nyctalope vs. Lucifer* (1921). One might be tempted to see this book as a "reboot" of the series, but later, in *La Captive du Démon* [*The Captive of the Demon*] (1927), when Sylvie MacDhul first meets Leo, she recognizes him as "the hero behind the exploration of planet Mars" and the man "who defeated the monster known as Lucifer," thereby firmly keeping the earlier volumes in the series.

Jean de La Hire was notoriously dismissive of his own continuity, and yet, by the time he decided to write the origins of the Nyctalope in 1933, he realized that his character was a somewhat unlikely 56 year-old hero in an unaging 40 year-old body.

Therefore, in *Enter the Nyctalope*, La Hire decided to move Leo's life-story forward in time by 15 years, stating that he was 20 in 1912, meaning that he was born in 1892, not in 1877 as previously established.

Another casual dismissal of previously established continuity was that Leo's father, who until then had been called Jean, and had been a French Navy Ensign and a diplomat, was now called Pierre and was a scientist.

To reconcile the events of *Enter the Nyctalope* with the books that came before it, one is forced to relocate its events to 1897, despite any topical references. It is possible to speculate that one of the unintended consequences of Doctor de Villiers-Pagan's radical heart surgery was to extend Leo's natural life-span, hence the necessity to enlist La Hire, Leo's biographer, to pretend that the Nyctalope was born later than he really was in order to not attract public attention.

Strangely, as Leo is about to die, having already suffered from a night of torture (p. 149), he is said to experience a vision of "eternal life" which may be an expression of religious belief, or a precognitive experience of what the future has in store for him.

The other two works warranting inclusion in the Nyctalope's bibliography are:

* *Le Trésor dans l'Abîme* [The Treasure of the Abyss], serialized in *L'Echo de Paris* (1906-07), reprinted in book form by Boivin in 1907, Rouff in 1922, and Tallandier, 1936). In this novel, which takes place from 1900 to 1907, John Dogg, an American millionaire, seeks to find a sunken treasure and, in order to do so, breaks the mad scientist Maur Korridès out from the asy-

lum where he was kept. Korridès designs a deep sea diving vehicle made of *heliose*, a synthetic substance of his own invention. Heliose is somewhat similar to cavorite, in that it repels, or is attracted by, various natural forces. Eventually, as the two partners reach their goal, they discover that gold causes heliose to become unstable. Dogg perishes in the ensuing explosion, and Korridès is believed to have died as well. We then discover in an epilog that Korridès and his wife, Marguerite Dormach, did not perish at the end of the novel, but found refuge, under a secret identity, in America. Several years later, Korridès built a new *heliose* sphere and he and Marguerite went to Mars.[13]

* *Les Chasseurs de Mystère* [*The Mystery Hunters*], serialized in *Le Matin* (1932) and reprinted as two books, *Les Chasseurs de Mystère* and *La Mort... L'Amour* [*Death... Love*] byFayard in 1933. In this novel, which takes place in 1932, we follow the adventures of Rex Sainclair, a.k.a. The Kleptomorph, who has the power to mimic the appearance of any man he chooses. Rex is trying to prevent a second World War, but his megalomaniacal methods, such as the assembling of an advanced fleet of pirate airplanes, have turned him into a villain in the eyes of the world. The so-called "Mystery Hunters" are a team of detectives and adventurers sent to capture him. In the end, Rex is murdered by a German agent.

Leo has a brief cameo during the course of the novel. He is actually on Mars, for reasons left unexplained

---

[13] A story by Emmanuel Gorlier untangling the various mysteries associated with Korridès and his son, Hugues Mézarek, a.k.a. Belzebuth, will be published in *Tales of the Shadowmen 6: Grand-Guignol* (ISBN 978-1-934543-90-0) in 2010.

(further exploration? Visiting the grave of his first wife Xaviere?) and is contacted via space radio by Jean de La Hire himself, who wants to know if Rex Sainclair is related to him. Leo denies it vehemently. Whether he is telling the truth remains unknown.

Finally, two corrections to our previous article:

We had written: "After *Les Mystères de Lyon*, neither Sylvie nor Pierre (either of them) ever makes a reappearance. Leo behaves as if he is single again, although he does not remarry. One is led to wonder if the couple separated, possibly because of the Nyctalope's continued infidelities." *Le Sphinx du Maroc* makes it clear that Sylvie died three years prior, i.e.: in 1931, and that Leo is a widower again.

We also noted that *"L'Enfant perdu [The Lost Child]* tells of an adventure that the Nyctalope and Gnô Mitang experienced during the June 1940 exodus after France was invaded by the Nazis." The Nyctalope and his friend do witness the kidnapping of the child by gypsies in 1940, but the story really ends in 1942 when they free the boy with the help of a young gypsy girl.

Jean-Marc Lofficier

cured by Professor Krausse. He was, in fact, released as the result of a general amnesty. As for the Professor, he had left Germany several years ago and was now wanted for various crimes, in which, however, his involvement had never been formally proved.

The German police requested that Dickson ask the British authorities to detain him, pending extradition proceedings that would be forthcoming swiftly.

"I confess that I was seduced by the man's vast intelligence," confessed Dickson later to Tom Wills. "He seemed to be such an outstanding scientist... But I made a mistake and was misled. Let he who is without sin cast the first stone!"

However, Dickson's mind was firmly made up: he intended to find Professor Krausse at all cost.

# CHAPTER TWO
## The Disappearance of Lady Bailey

Harry Dickson was convinced that Professor Krausse was still in London, and the information he had received from the German police only supported that notion.

When he asked the Germans for more information about the Professor's past, however, they weren't as forthcoming and became quite reticent. Krausse had been accused of conducting various human experiments, but without details; he was also accused of fraud, but without specifics as to his victims.

*A man like him*, thought the detective, *is bound to gravitate towards the medical establishments. I'll keep an eye on hospitals, clinics and morgues...*

Dickson managed to convince Scotland Yard to assist him in the matter, and was able to set up a surveillance network of such places, but the reports he received remained resolutely negative. Professor Krausse and his murdering protégé seemed to have vanished in the legendary fog of London...

As it sometimes happened, luck suddenly stepped into the void, offering the detective a tiny clue that was the beginning of a trail.

That clue was a car accident involving Lady Helen Bailey, a notorious London beauty who had attended the performance of a popular play at a theater in Drury Lane, and was returning home to her Brickley estate in her

Rolls Royce when, suddenly, near Peckham Rye Commons, her car was hit by a lorry.

The lorry fled the site of the accident, but the Rolls, seriously damaged, was immobilized. Worse, Lady Helen had been severely shocked during the collision.

Her driver, panicking, asked the few passers-by for the address of the closest doctor. He was informed by a Good Samaritan that there was one in a nearby street, just across from Scylla Road. It was indeed very close and, with the help of the man, the driver was able to take Lady Helen to that address.

It was a sad little house, newly built but already looking somewhat dilapidated. There was a brass plate next to the door that advertised that it was the surgery of a Doctor Lengorski.

The driver had to ring several times before someone answered. Doctor Lengorski was a thickly-built man who spoke with a marked Eastern European accent.

He didn't seem very pleased at being disturbed at such a late hour, but yielded to the driver's loud pleas for help, supported by those of the indignant Good Samaritan. So he invited them in, still grumbling, and took them into a poorly-equipped consultation room.

There, the doctor examined Lady Helen, stopped the bleeding which had started, then, in light of her weakened state, declared that she shouldn't be transported. He said that Lady Helen could stay in his surgery until the morning, at which time decisions about further care could be made.

The driver asked to call her husband, but Doctor Lengorski didn't have a telephone, so the man had to return home to Brockley on foot to tell his employer what had happened. Unfortunately, that evening, Sir Morton had been urgently summoned to the side of one of his aunts, who had been taken ill. He had left a note for his wife to tell her not to expect him back until the next day.

The driver, exhausted, decided that there was nothing mire he could do, and went to bed.

He was still asleep the following morning when a taxi stopped before the mansion and let Sir Morton out. He was in a very foul mood, for it turned out that the telegram he had received was fake, and that his aunt was in excellent health. He thought that he had been the butt of some kind of practical joke.

When the driver told him about the accident of the previous night, and his wife's condition, Sir Morton was understandably alarmed and he and his man immediately returned to Peckham Rye Commons. They reached Scylla Road, then the house of Doctor Lengorski, and rang the bell.

No one answered.

Sir Morton then made such a ruckus, banging on the door and shouting, that he woke up the neighbors. They said they barely knew Lengorski, who had moved in only a couple of weeks earlier. Sir Morton asked them to call the police, who sent a constable with the authorization to enter Lengorski's house by force if necessary.

The policeman broke down the door, but they didn't find anyone inside. The bloodied rags used to staunch Lady Helen's bleeding the night before were still in the surgery, but there were no traces of her, or of Lengorski.

They searched the house, which turned out to be totally empty, with curtains to make it look as if someone lived there, but no items of furniture. In front of the house, the police found a spot of motor oil, indicating that a car had parked there recently.

The next day, the story of the elusive and mysterious Doctor Lengorski made the rounds at Scotland Yard and was in the morning papers. The inspector in charge of the case asked Harry Dickson for his help.

When the detective arrived, he first asked to take a look at the Baileys' Rolls Royce, which was still parked where it had been left after the accident.

"Hmm... A tank could hardly have done a better job," said Dickson, after he had finished examining the car. "Look at the damage: no traces of paint or metal scrapings from the other vehicle; this was not a sideswipe, but a front end collision. This car was rammed on purpose."

"So you don't think it was an accident?" asked the Inspector, flabbergasted.

"Not in the least," replied Dickson sharply.

"But... If that's so... My wife being taken to that strange doctor..." stammered Sir Morton who had been attending the investigation.

"All part of an ingenious set-up, I'm afraid," said the detective. "Your wife wounded, a helpful Good Samaritan, a neighboring doctor..." Dickson turned towards the driver. "Please describe to me in detail what these two men looked like: the Good Samaritan and Doctor Lengorski."

"Well, the man who offered his help was big and strong; he was able to lift and carry Lady Morton effortlessly. I don't remember his face very well; besides, he wore a broad-rimmed hat. He spoke with a posh accent, but he wasn't particularly well dressed. As for the doctor, he was a smaller man, with an awkward step. He had a rather unkempt large beard. He seemed rather strong too, although he stooped a little. His surgery was badly lit, with only a small bulb powered by a battery. I don't think the house had electricity; I only saw a candle in the entry hall."

They then moved to Lengorski's house. Dickson examined the surgery, furnished with a few, second-hand supplies.

"Pah! The whole lot isn't worth ten pounds," he remarked.

In the courtyard behind the house, the detective noticed a sewer grate which had recently been opened, because its coating of rust and crud had been scratched away. He removed it and, with a cane, started fishing through the foul-smelling mud at the bottom. Quickly, he found what he was looking for and pulled up a slimy mass of hair trickling with dirty water.

"Doctor Lengorski couldn't have found a better place to get rid of his fake beard," he snickered.

The search of the remaining floors of the house turned up nothing except for some ashes in one of the fireplaces.

"Old newspapers..." muttered Dickson. "That's more like it..." Kneeling down, the detective began to scrutinize the charred fragments with a magnifying glass. "Gothic typeface... German newspapers... The ashes alone prove it..."

"I think that the bandits who kidnapped Lady Bailey will soon ask for a ransom," said the Inspector.

Dickson said nothing, because the notion had just occurred to him that Professor Krausse might well be behind this disappearance; certainly, the description the driver had given of Lengorski could have fit the German doctor.

In any event, in the following days, Sir Morton received no ransom demands, and Lady Helen remained unfindable, despite all the manpower that Scotland Yard assigned to the case.

# CHAPTER THREE
## A Trap… And a Conversation

"We must start again from the beginning," said Dickson, "and that means with the first element in this case, which is the man, Schwertfeger.

"What do we know about him? According to appearances, he is nothing but a vulgar criminal, a German sailor wandering aimlessly around the London wharves. He was discovered in a back alley of Limehouse bent over the still warm body of one of his compatriots. He was seen in company of the victim the day before the murder, doing the rounds of the local pubs, encouraging his companion to drink more than reasonable.

"The victim was a man in his 20s, strong and sturdy; Schwertfeger, on the other hand, is older and his face shows the ravages of vice. He didn't put up any resistance when he was arrested, and didn't put up any defense when he was tried and sentenced to hang…"

Dickson looked at the photographs before him, which he had obtained from Scotland Yard: they showed a tallish man with a blank, ordinary face, partially hidden behind an untrimmed, bushy beard.

The detective used all his influence to pressure the *Kriminal Abteilung* in Berlin to send him more information, and eventually received the visit of a Herr Doktor Mendel, sent especially from Berlin to talk to him.

Dickson became immediately aware that the German was trying to buy his silence about Schwertfeger and Professor Krausse, and convince him to drop the case. They were at an impasse.

But then the detective suddenly remembered his first encounter with the Professor in Berlin in 1919, and was inspired to pursue his inquiry in that direction.

"Wasn't Herr Professor Krausse somehow involved in the sinister scandal of the human meat traffickers of *Nachtrabengasse*?" he abruptly asked Mendel.

"How could you know that?" replied the German, taken aback.

The detective hadn't known it for certain, but was pleased to see his suspicions confirmed.

Eventually, the German reluctantly told him the full story.

"Well, yes, even though we never had any hard evidence. No one wanted to talk, even at the feet of the scaffold, and then, well, Professor Krausse was an important man... There would have been much embarrassment... So we suggested that he should leave Germany and never return."

"Did he comply?"

"Well, mostly... I mean..."

"You mean that he returned occasionally to take care of various businesses, none of which were particularly honest?"

"*Donnerwetter, Mein Herr!* Please don't go spreading such rumors. My superiors in Berlin would be very unhappy."

"Have no fear, *Mein Herr*, I'm only interested in what the eminent Professor came to England to do. What connection is there between Krausse and Schwertfeger?"

"I confess we don't know that ourselves," admitted Mendel, "but Professor Krausse is known to frequent some very disreputable characters."

"Is he attracted to money?"

"No."

"Honors?"

"Even less! He has, in fact, always behaved very rudely towards the highest members of German society."

"What, then, is his primary motivation?"

"Science, we believe."

"Yes, but which branch of science?"

"Anatomy, perhaps. He is the author of some remarkable monographs in the field, even though they remained unpublished because of his rather extravagant theories about the human brain."

"If Scotland Yard was to arrest Professor Krausse and extradite him to Germany, as you proposed, what would you do with him? Would you try him in a Court of Law."

There was a brief flash in Herr Mendel's icy blue eyes.

"We would certainly prevent him from causing any more harm," he replied cautiously.

"Meaning that you wouldn't hesitate to get rid of him?"

Herr Mendel said nothing, but the expression on his face spoke volumes.

"Very well," said Dickson finally. "I suppose you must have your reasons, and that they must be good ones. As it turns out, I might be of some assistance…"

"Germany knows how to reward those who help her," interrupted the envoy from Friedrichstrasse.

"Not so fast! We're not there yet, Herr Mendel. You'll have to trust me, which so far, you haven't done. I'm going to ask you a very important question, and I want a truthful answer. Was Professor Krausse working alone?"

"What do you mean?" said Mendel weakly. "What do you know exactly?"

"I thought I was being clear. Professor Krausse had only disdain for money; he wasn't rich, he lived modestly…"

"That is true."

"…And yet, scientific experiments cost money, often a great deal of money. So did he have a patron, a benefactor? Someone who paid for his lab equipment?"

"He did," admitted Mendel, lowering his voice. "An American. Someone who found his way to Berlin after the War and whom Krausse must have met right after the Armistice. His name—or the name he used—was Wentcroft. We were never able to get any information about him, or his past."

"As regards the Affair of the *Nachtrabengasse*, you had the facts suppressed because of Krausse's involvement, am I correct?"

"You are. The Professor still enjoyed some pretty powerful political connections."

"But he did it again, didn't he? I mean, you discovered other cases of human flesh trafficking in which he was involved, right?"

"Yes, you're right, Mister Dickson. You clearly understand this appalling business."

"And I suppose that Wentcroft's dollars bought the impunity which the Professor appeared to enjoy, through bribes and other payments made under the table?"

Mendel lowered his head in shame.

"Please describe this Wentcroft character, Herr Mendel."

The German made a gesture of impotence.

"He is a clever devil! Our agents were never able to get a good look at him. He is tall with long hair and a red beard—not at all looking like an American."

"Hmm. He could have been wearing a wig and a false beard," said Dickson.

"We thought of that as well."

Harry Dickson then smiled in a mysterious fashion.

"Are you planning to stay in London for long, Herr Mendel?" he asked.

"Another week at least, Mister Dickson. I have other matters to discuss at Scotland Yard."

"Excellent. A week should be more than enough time. Before you return to Berlin, will you please call on me again?"

The second person to visit Harry Dickson that day was the unfortunate Sir Morton Bailey. The loss of his wife had gravely affected him. He had aged prodigiously in a matter of days. He was now stooped, his eyes were lifeless, and he spoke in a slow and dull voice.

"Sir Morton," started the detective, "I asked you to come here because I have a few questions to which I need answers. I hope you will have the strength to provide such answers, even though some of my questions might prove embarrassing, and possibly even painful?"

"It no longer matters, Mister Dickson. Now that my life is over, you can ask me anything you want. I doubt I will care about any potential embarrassment."

"Very well. Let me begin by observing that there are a few years of difference in age between you and Lady Bailey…"

"You are being kind, Sir. Lady Helen was—is, I still hope—in her late 30s, and as beautiful as she was in her 20s, while I have just passed 60. Nevertheless, our marriage is strong and a model of its kind."

The detective didn't have the heart to contradict the unfortunate husband, for it was known in the capital that

Lady Helen had, in fact, had several affairs. But as is always the case, the husband was the only one unaware of that fact.

"Lady Bailey wasn't British, I gather?"

"Correct. I met her in Germany. She belonged to a very respectable and distinguished family from Hanover, small-time aristocrats ruined by the War."

"And you married her in Berlin?"

"Yes. At the time, I was working there for the British Commission on Reparations."

"Have you ever heard of a Professor Krausse?"

"Krausse, you say?... No, I don't think so. But Helen was a student at Berlin University when I first made her acquaintance."

"Was she a medical student?"

"Perhaps. Or Natural Sciences... After our engagement, which was very short, she of course stopped all her studies."

"You don't recall her mentioning one of her professors by that name?"

"I'm afraid not. I'm not a scientist, Mister Dickson, and I have little knowledge about science. I've traveled much, but not learned a great deal in that respect. My conversations with Helen were rarely about abstract matters."

"Did you travel a lot recently, and did you leave your wife alone in London?"

"Well, I had to go to America several times, on a particularly delicate matter concerning the trade relationship between our country and the United States. But is this all really relevant? Have you nothing new to tell me about my poor, unfortunate Helen?"

"Actually, I do," said Dickson in such a strong, matter-of-fact tone that Sir Morton was taken aback. "I know where she is right now."

"What? But how?... Please tell me, Mister Dickson?"

"Right now, she's at home in Brockley."

"At home? I don't understand?"

"She's about to leave in the company of an American gentleman named Wentcroft."

Suddenly, Sir Morton let out a growl not unlike that of a wounded beast.

"Wentcroft?" he shouted. "Really? Wentcroft! What kind of game are you playing at, Dickson?"

"Don't you think you're the one who's been playing games, Sir Morton?" said Dickson coolly. "And I'm afraid that you've lost."

Sir Morton now looked like a wild beast at bay, desperately looking for any avenue of escape. He clenched his fists and stared at the detective, with murder in his eyes.

"Don't make a foolish move, Sir Morton," said Dickson, calmly unveiling a revolver, which he had carefully kept hidden in his sleeve. "Or I won't be able to save you from the gallows a second time."

This time, Sir Morton collapsed back into his chair. His eyes became strangely fixed, looking into the distance with a glassy stare.

Harry Dickson rang a bell and Tom Wills entered.

"Tom, please go down into the street. You'll find a German gentleman in an overcoat and a floppy hat pacing back and forth on the opposite sidewalk. Ask him to come up."

Soon, Tom returned with Herr Mendel in tow.

"Good day, Herr Mendel. I thought you might want to pursue your own investigation by spying on me. I don't blame you for trying. In fact, it made it easier for me to find you. Please take a look at this gentleman, portray him wearing a red wig and a beard, and tell me if he reminds you of someone?"

"*Herr im Himmel!*" exclaimed the German policeman. "It's Wentcroft!"

"Indeed. But more importantly, it's also Sir Morton Bailey, who was forced to leave Her Majesty's service in Malaysia because he was suspected of cannibalistic practices, which he had been indulging in after joining some kind of secret, local cult. Undoubtedly, a man of great worth, but also totally, incurably mad. No, don't be concerned; he can't hear what we're saying. He's quite catatonic."

"What are you going to do now?" asked Mendel, stammering.

"I'm going to ask you to please inform your friends, Herr Professor Krausse and Lady Bailey, that they no longer have anything to fear from this monster, and that they should come here and talk to me in safety."

# EPILOGUE

Herr Mendel used the telephone and, barely an hour later, the doorbell rang.

"Herr Professor Krausse," said Harry Dickson, offering his hand to the old man standing on the threshold. "I'm glad to see you without your carnavalesque disguise—and you too, Lady Bailey."

"That accursed name!' muttered the scientist. "As soon as we're back in Berlin, she'll return to using her maiden name…"

"Helen Krausse," said Dickson, "since she is your daughter."

"I'll explain…"

"No need to, my dear Professor, In fact, please allow me to tell the story, and correct me if I'm wrong. It will be educational for Tom, my assistant."

"Where's Morton?" asked Krausse.

"Back in Bedlam, this time for the rest of his natural life. As you know, he truly is mad."

"I knew it, of course. But what a genius too."

"So here is the story… After the War, you, Professor, found yourself in Berlin with scant resources. You were too proud to ask for help. Then you met a very wealthy Englishman, Sir Morton Bailey, who seemed to share your interest in anatomy and was willing to finance your research. Sir Morton then met your daughter, Helen, who was also your assistant. He courted and married her; you didn't object despite the difference in their ages, because he was rich and titled, and you wanted Helen to enjoy a secure position in life. It was only afterward, and by pure chance, that you discovered your new son-in-law's ghastly secret: during his stay in Malaysia, he had become a cannibal! He liked the taste of human flesh! When I first met you at that tavern in the *Nachtrabengasse*, you were following Sir Morton, trying to protect your daughter and spare her the awful discovery. After the scandal broke, you forced him to return to England, but because it was easier to satisfy his vice in post-war Germany, he returned several times, using the alias of Wentcroft.

"In the underworld of Berlin, he created another alias for himself: that of the sailor Schwertferger, a real man who had been recently relesaed from prison, and whom Morton killed to take his place. Eventually, Germany became as dangerous a place for him as England, so he resigned himself to spending more time as Sir Morton Bailey in London, with his beautiful young wife, who still knew nothing about his awful double-life.

"But eventually, his luck changed. He was arrested in London for the murder of another sailor while he was using Schwertferger's identity. You couldn't stand the idea that the husband of your daughter was going to hang on the gallows, so you contacted me to have him committed instead, and later arranged for his escape. But there, you made a mistake: you told Morton you knew his secret and threatened to reveal everything to Helen if he didn't mend his ways. Then she would surely leave him and detest him forever.

"You realized your mistake at once, of course. If Morton couldn't keep Helen, he was prepared to kill her. So you assumed the identity of Doctor Lengorski and kept an eye on the couple. One night, Morton tried to kill his wife, crashing into her car with a lorry. Fortunately, a Good Samaritan intervened and carried Helen to Lengorski's surgery. That kind soul who had been following the couple, ready to act as per your instructions, Professor, was of course you, Herr Mendel..."

Harry Dickson stopped and tipped his head to the German policeman.

"Berlin hadn't forgotten that Professor Krausse had once been a good and loyal servitor of the State and had dispatched one of their best men to help him."

Herr Mendel almost blushed.

"I deserve no praise, Mister Dickson," he said, "because I never pierced the secret of Sir Morton's other identities. In all fairness, however, my orders were strictly limited to helping the Professor and his daughter."

"And you succeeded very well in that mission."

"You, however, solved the case and exposed the monster."

"I believe you would have done just as well, Herr Mendel, had our positions been reversed. I spoke an hour with you and I'm a good judge of character, and I could tell that you were a tireless policeman under your assumed bureaucratic façade. Then, when I talked to Sir Morton, it was not difficult to detect the madness that lurked just beneath the surface. It only took one word to expose him: Wentcroft. He thought for a minute that Professor Krausse had become Wentcroft to steal Helen, or perhaps that Wentcroft had somehow become real... Who can tell with madmen? The rest was child's play. And I'm very pleased to conclude my tale by saying that, from the very beginning, I always felt that Professor Krausse was a good and decent man who could be trusted, despite all appearances and every accusation thrown at him. And I'm glad to see that I was right, and that is reward enough for my efforts!"

## SF & FANTASY

Guy d'Armen. *Doc Ardan: The City of Gold and Lepers*
G.-J. Arnaud. *The Ice Company*
Aloysius Bertrand. *Gaspard de la Nuit*
Richard Bessière. *The Gardens of the Apocalypse*
Félix Bodin. *The Novel of the Future*
André Caroff. *The Terror of Madame Atomos*
Didier de Chousy. *Ignis*
Captain Danrit. *Undersea Odyssey*
C. I. Defontenay. *Star (Psi Cassiopeia)*
Charles Derennes. *The People of the Pole*
Georges Dodds/Paul Wessels (anthologists). *The Missing Link*
Harry Dickson. *The Heir of Dracula*
Jules Dornay. *Lord Ruthven Begins*
Sâr Dubnotal *vs. Jack the Ripper*
Alexandre Dumas. *The Return of Lord Ruthven*
J.-C. Dunyach. *The Night Orchid; The Thieves of Silence*
Henri Duvernois. *The Man Who Found Himself*
Henri Falk. *The Age of Lead*
Paul Féval. *Anne of the Isles; Knightshade; Revenants; Vampire City; The Vampire Countess; The Wandering Jew's Daughter*
Paul Féval, *fils. Felifax, the Tiger-Man*
Arnould Galopin. *Doctor Omega*
G.L. Gick. *Harry Dickson: The Werewolf of Rutherford Grange*
Nathalie Henneberg. *The Green Gods*
V. Hugo, P. Foucher & P. Meurice. *The Hunchback of Notre-Dame*
Michel Jeury. *Chronolysis*
Octave Joncquel & Theo Varlet. *The Martian Epic*
Gérard Klein. *The Mote in Time's Eye*
Jean de La Hire. *Enter the Nyctalope; The Nyctalope on Mars; The Nyctalope vs. Lucifer*
André Laurie. *Spiridon*
Georges Le Faure & Henri de Graffigny. *The Extraordinary Adventures of a Russian Scientist Across the Solar System* (2 vols.)
Gustave Le Rouge. *The Vampires of Mars*
Jules Lermina. *Mysteryville; Panic in Paris; To-Ho and the Gold Destroyers*
Jean-Marc & Randy Lofficier. *Edgar Allan Poe on Mars; The Katrina Protocol; Pacifica; Robonocchio; Tales of the Shadowmen* (anthologists; 7 vols.)
Xavier Mauméjean. *The League of Heroes*

John-Antoine Nau. *Enemy Force*
Marie Nizet. *Captain Vampire*
C. Nodier, A. Beraud & Toussaint-Merle. *Frankenstein*
Henri de Parville. *An Inhabitant of the Planet Mars*
J. Polidori, C. Nodier, E. Scribe. *Lord Ruthven the Vampire*
P.-A. Ponson du Terrail. *The Vampire and the Devil's Son*
Maurice Renard. *The Blue Peril; Doctor Lerne; The Doctored Man;.
A Man Among the Microbes; The Master of Light*
Albert Robida. *The Adventures of Saturnin Farandoul; The Clock of
the Centuries.*
J.-H. Rosny Aîné. *Helgvor of the Blue River; The Givreuse Enigma;
The Mysterious Force; The Navigators of Space; Vamireh; The
World of the Variants; The Young Vampire*
Han Ryner. *The Superhumans*
Brian Stableford. *The New Faust at the Tragicomique;The Empire of
the Necromancers (The Shadow of Frankenstein; Frankenstein and
the Vampire Countess; Frankenstein in London); Sherlock Holmes &
The Vampires of Eternity; The Stones of Camelot; The Wayward
Muse.* (anthologist) *The Germans on Venus; News from the Moon;
The Supreme Progress*
Jacques Spitz. *The Eye of Purgatory*
Kurt Steiner. *Ortog*
Villiers de l'Isle-Adam. *The Scaffold; The Vampire Soul*
Philippe Ward. *Artahe*
Philippe Ward & Sylvie Miller. *The Song of Montségur*

## MYSTERIES & THRILLERS
M. Allain & P. Souvestre. *The Daughter of Fantômas*
A. Anicet-Bourgeois, Lucien Dabril. *Rocambole*
A. Bisson & G. Livet. *Nick Carter vs. Fantômas*
V. Darlay & H. de Gorsse. *Lupin vs. Holmes: The Stage Play*
Paul Féval. *Gentlemen of the Night; John Devil; The Black Coats
('Salem Street; The Invisible Weapon; The Parisian Jungle; The
Companions of the Treasure; Heart of Steel; The Cadet Gang)*
Emile Gaboriau. *Monsieur Lecoq*
Steve Leadley. *Sherlock Holmes: The Circle of Blood*
Maurice Leblanc. *Arsène Lupin vs. Countess Cagliostro; Lupin vs.
Holmes (The Blonde Phantom; The Hollow Needle)*
Gaston Leroux. *Chéri-Bibi; The Phantom of the Opera; Rouletabille
& the Mystery of the Yellow Room*
William Patrick Maynard. *The Terror of Fu Manchu*

Frank J. Morlock. *Sherlock Holmes: The Grand Horizontals*
P. de Wattyne & Y. Walter. *Sherlock Holmes vs. Fantômas*
David White. *Fantômas in America*

## SCREENPLAYS

Mike Baron. *The Iron Triangle*
Emma Bull & Will Shetterly. *Nightspeeder; War for the Oaks*
Gerry Conway & Roy Thomas. *Doc Dynamo*
Steve Englehart. *Majorca*
James Hudnall. *The Devastator*
Jean-Marc & Randy Lofficier. *Royal Flush*
J.-M. & R. Lofficier & Marc Agapit. *Despair*
Andrew Paquette. *Peripheral Vision*
R. Thomas, J. Hendler & L. Sprague de Camp. *Rivers of Time*

## NON-FICTION

Stephen R. Bissette. *Blur 1-5. Green Mountain Cinema 1*
Win Scott Eckert. *Crossovers* (2 vols.)
Jean-Marc & Randy Lofficier. *Shadowmen* (2 vols.)
Randy Lofficier. *Over Here*

## HEXAGON COMICS

Franco Frescura & Luciano Bernasconi. *Wampus*
Franco Frescura & Giorgio Trevisan. *CLASH*
L. Bernasconi, J.-M. Lofficier & Juan Roncagliolo Berger. *Phenix*
Claude Legrand, J.-M. Lofficier & L. Bernasconi. *Kabur*
Franco Oneta. *Zembla*
L. Buffolente, Lofficier & J.-J. Dzialowski. *Strangers: Homicron*
Danilo Grossi. *Strangers: Jaydee*
Claude Legrand & Luciano Bernasconi. *Strangers: Starlock*

## ART BOOKS

Jean-Pierre Normand. *Science Fiction Illustrations*
Raven Okeefe. *Raven's L'il Critters*
Randy Lofficier & Raven OKeefe. *If Your Possum Go Daylight...*
Daniele Serra. *Illusions*